SAMPLER

Sampler

Fifty Short Stories
by

DON TASSONE

BOOKS

Adelaide Books
New York / Lisbon
2019

SAMPLER

Fifty Short Stories

By Don Tassone

Published by Adelaide Books, New York / Lisbon
adelaidebooks.org

Editor-in-Chief
Stevan V. Nikolic

For any information, please address Adelaide Books
at info@adelaidebooks.org

or write to:

Adelaide Books
244 Fifth Ave. Suite D27
New York, NY, 10001

ISBN-10: 1-951214-60-9

ISBN-13: 978-1-951214-60-9

Printed in the United States of America

For my children

Contents

Acknowledgements

I want to thank my wife, Liz, Kathy Kennedy, Christine des Garennes, Andi Rogers, Anna Gayford, Murray Bodo and Christine Sneed for their helpful feedback on various stories in this collection.

I also want to extend grateful acknowledgement to the editors of the online literary magazines where the original versions of many of these stories appeared: *TWJ Magazine, 101 Words, Flash Fiction Magazine, Down in the Dirt, Friday Flash Fiction, Page & Spine, Literary Yard, Edify Fiction, Mused* and *Red Fez.*

Don Tassone

Preface

Conventional wisdom holds that story collections should have a theme. In this way, this book is unconventional.

The 50 stories in this collection are wide-ranging. Some are serious, others light. Most are gentle, but a few are disquieting. There is fantasy, spirituality and politics here.

"Mother Earth" is a sequel to a story called "Walk in the Grass," which was featured in my second story collection. "Snow" is a prose poem. "Flashpoint" is non-fiction.

Many of these stories are slices of life. Most are short. All are an invitation to think more deeply.

I hope you enjoy this diverse assortment of stories.

Don Tassone
January 2019

Late Bloomer

Three miles into his daily run, on a crisp morning in early October, he began to ask himself why he'd waited so long to begin exercising this way.

He wondered about the toll on his body from being out-of-shape so long. He wondered how many more years he might have if he'd taken better care of himself sooner.

The leaves had either changed or fallen. Along the forest floor, he spotted a patch of yellow wildflowers, which were just blooming. How grateful he felt to see such a splash of color, just now, amidst the browning autumn palette.

Simple Dream

"Are you happy?" he asked.

"Yes," she said, sipping her coffee. "Are you?"

They were sitting at opposite ends of the sofa, facing each other, their legs outstretched. It was a chilly morning, and they shared a blanket. She pulled it up, nearly to her neck, leaving him just enough to cover his legs, but he didn't mind.

Some men dream of fame and fortune. But for years, he had dreamed of waking up when he wanted, with nowhere to go, and sharing quiet mornings with the woman he loved.

"Very," he answered, smiling and sipping his coffee too.

Bird

She sat nestled in her baby seat, looking out the back window.

A robin lighted on a stone wall. The baby watched the bird jerk its head around and then fly away. It filled her with wonder.

A year later, she stood at the same window. Again, she saw a robin.

"Bird," her mother said.

"Bird," the toddler repeated.

Some years later, the girl pulled open her back door and sprang outside. The noise startled a small flock of robins perched in a sugar maple, and the birds flew off.

But the girl didn't notice as she ran next door to play.

When You're 10

Awakened by the sun, he lay there for a moment, worried he was late for school. Then he remembered it was the first day of summer vacation.

For a 10-year-old boy, what could be better? Waking up late, eating Frosted Flakes, playing baseball, stopping home for lunch, fishing, heading home for supper and watching TV until bedtime.

When you're 10, you can venture out on your own. You don't care what you wear or pay much attention to girls. You don't have a job.

All summer vacations are a blast, but none can match the one when you're 10.

Listen

Clara awoke in the near darkness. She strained her ears but could hear nothing. She peeled back her covers, got out of bed and stepped carefully down the hallway, touching the plaster wall with her fingertips to guide her way.

She reached a doorway and went in. A nightlight cast a faint glow about the nursery. Clara went over to the crib and leaned down to get a good look at her infant son. He appeared to be sleeping. She stared at his face and chest, eager to see him breathe. He stirred, and she breathed a sigh of relief.

She reached down, smoothed his hair and held the side of his face in her hand. Then she went back to bed and slept for another hour before she woke up and did the same thing again.

★

For the first two years of her life, Clara had the hearing of a normal child. But just before her third birthday, she contracted meningitis. It nearly killed her. Over many months, her health was restored, but she lost most of her hearing.

It was a time before most people, especially children, wore hearing aids. Clara went to school with the other kids, but there was no special education for children with disabilities.

Nearly deaf, she had a hard time keeping up and was labeled a "slow learner."

Clara was 16 before she graduated from the eighth grade. School had been so difficult and frustrating that she decided not to go to high school. Instead, she got a job selling men's clothing in a local department store.

One day, she met Henry there. He had just graduated from high school and come in to buy a suit because he had just accepted a sales position with a local paper company. Clara was taken by his smile and careful way of speaking. She could read his lips. It was as if he knew about her.

She asked Henry what type of suit he was looking for and showed him the store's offerings. As she described the various styles, he listened to her carefully and watched her closely. She had never had a man pay so much attention to her. She liked that.

She helped Henry pick out a suit and a shirt and tie to match, and a tailor took his measurements. Clara walked past the open entrance to the fitting room and saw Henry standing on a wooden platform, with the tailor on his knees, marking the hem of his pants. She didn't mean to stare, but Henry looked so handsome in his brown, double-breasted suit. He spotted her in the trifold mirror and smiled. She blushed and hurried back to the cash register, but she was glad she had seen him that way.

Before he left the store, Henry introduced himself to Clara. He extended his hand, and she took it. Something felt so right to her about holding his hand.

He came back a week later to pick up his new suit. Clara knew when it would be ready and made sure she was working that day. Seeing Henry again made her feel warm inside and a little dizzy.

As she rung up his order, Henry asked Clara if she would like to have dinner. She could hardly believe he had asked that and thought she might have misheard him.

"Pardon me?" she said.

"I said would you like to have dinner sometime?"

"I would love to," she said, smiling.

A year later, Clara and Henry were married. A year after that, their first child, a boy, was born.

★

Henry was a wonderful husband and a doting father. He also happened to be a very heavy sleeper, and he seldom woke up at night when his children were babies. Getting up with the children at night was a role Clara would play.

Over 15 years, they had seven children. When each of them was a baby, Clara woke up nearly every hour at night to check on her newborn. She couldn't hear if they were crying, and she had to be sure they were all right.

She would examine them closely in their crib to make sure they were breathing. Sometimes, they would be crying, and she would pick them up and hold them, feed them, sing to them. Sometimes, she would pick them up even if they were sleeping just to hold them and feel them fall asleep again in her arms.

Even when her children were no longer infants, Clara would check on them at night. Thus, as everyone else in the house was asleep, Clara was tiptoeing from room to room, keeping watch over her children.

As a result, she got precious little sleep herself. Over time, this took a great toll on her. She aged rapidly. At 25, Clara looked 40. When she turned 30, her hair had begun to turn gray and her face was wrinkled.

Henry grew concerned. He begged Clara to get more rest, but she always waved him off.

"I'm okay," she would say, "and I must know our children are okay too."

By her mid-40s, Clara began forgetting things. She developed tremors, and her speech became soft and slurred.

Henry insisted she see a doctor. Finally, she gave in. Tests showed she had Parkinson's Disease and dementia.

After that, her decline was rapid and steep. By the time she was 50, Clara was bedridden. Her doctor said there was little more he could do for her. He mentioned a nursing home, but Clara insisted on staying in her own home and implored Henry to keep her there.

"Of course," he said, holding her hand and kissing her cheek.

Her need for care was nearly constant now. Henry was still working, so each of their children, all of them now adults, took turns caring for their mother. They each took one day of the week. It was a full day too because they always woke up at night to check on her.

At last, Clara's body forgot how to swallow. For two days and two nights, Henry and all the children gathered around her. They were all with her the morning she stopped breathing.

★

It is said that God hears every leaf that falls in the forest. If that is true, it must be because every leaf is dear to him and he listens with his heart.

Pieces of Silver

The boy squatted to get a good look at an object shining in the grass. It was a silver dollar! He picked it up. He'd never held so much money in his hands.

He sprinted home to show everyone his newfound treasure.

With wide eyes, his little sister asked, "Can I have it?"

Without knowing why, he handed it to her.

She jumped up and down, waved her hands wildly and squealed with delight. He had never seen his sister so happy.

Now he's a wealthy man. Anonymously, he has bags of silver dollars delivered to schools in the poorer parts of town with instructions to give each child a coin.

He has never been inside these schools, but in his mind, he sees the smiling faces of the children there as they are each handed a silver dollar. He sees his sister's face, and he is happy.

Rest Stop Ghosts

I pulled into the parking space at the rest stop but couldn't open my door. The front door of a van parked next to me was wide open, inches from my door. A woman was standing on the running board, facing the back of the van, keeping close watch as her kids got out.

"Don't touch anything!" she yelled, as they ran toward the restrooms.

"Hurry up!" shouted a man standing on the other side of the van.

The scene reminded me of our family vacations when I was a kid. We traveled by station wagon. My dad was always hell-bent on getting to our destination. He would drive long stretches between stops, and we often took breaks at rest areas. Dad was always on us to hurry, and Mom was always telling us not to touch anything.

Stepping down from the running board, the woman next to me finally realized her door was blocking me from getting out.

"Oh, I'm sorry!" she said, closing it.

I smiled and opened my door.

"It's okay," I said. "I'm not in a hurry."

These rest areas used to creep me out. *How silly,* I thought.

Not that we spent much time there. We'd pull in, and Dad and one of my older brothers would grab a cooler out of the back of our station wagon and lug it to a picnic table. By the time they got there, Mom had already covered the top with a plastic tablecloth and was beginning to unpack the picnic basket.

Mom made us go to the bathroom and wash up both before *and* after lunch.

"Don't touch anything!" she would call after us.

"And hurry up!" Dad would add.

We hated going into those bathrooms. It seemed like there was always a creepy-looking guy in there mopping the floor. No matter the location of the rest stop, he always seemed to look the same, with a mustache and a baggy gray uniform.

"Watch your step," he would say in a gravelly voice.

Then there were the vending machines. They were usually lined up in a little cinderblock building with glass walls. My parents would never let us buy anything, but we'd always check out the offerings.

We never lingered at those rest stops. Mom and Dad were always eager to get back on the road, and we were okay with that. It always seemed there were strange-looking people lurking about. We never strayed far from my parents.

Now I grinned remembering it. *How childish to be so afraid,* I thought. As I stood at the urinal, I heard water dripping behind me. I looked around and saw a guy in a gray uniform pressing down on the handle on the top of a bucket, wringing water out of a mop.

Funny, I hadn't seen him when I came in.

"Watch your step," he said in a coarse voice, flopping the mop down on the floor.

He had a mustache.

I zipped up, ran water over my hands and got out of there. All of a sudden, I was worried about touching anything.

I still had a few hours of driving ahead of me, and I was tired, so I decided to grab a cup of coffee. The vending machines were in a small, cinderblock building. I stepped inside. I pulled a dollar bill out of my wallet, inserted it in the coffee machine and pressed the button.

As I waited for the coffee to dispense, I heard the door open. An overweight, bearded man stepped in. He was wearing a jeans jacket and a ball cap. Grunting, he waddled back and forth behind me. Then he stepped up to one of the candy machines and shoved his chubby finger into the metal slot for change. I grabbed my coffee and left.

Outside, people were shuffling along the sidewalks to and from the restrooms. Some were meandering in the grass. No one was saying a word. Everyone was moving slowly, like zombies.

A skeleton-thin man sat on the top of a picnic table, smoking a cigarette. A crow cawed. A dog, which looked like a wolf, started barking. The sky grew overcast. Thunder rolled in the distance. Out of nowhere, the wind kicked up, shaking tree limbs and rustling leaves.

I hurried back to my car, ducked inside and locked it. As I backed out, I could see the faces of dozens of people, all of them slightly swaying and looking my way. My headlights illuminated their eyes, which glowed like iridescent rosary beads.

I noticed the van was gone. In its place was an old Pontiac station wagon, just like the one my dad used to drive.

Natural Man

Bill Sykes always was a natural man.

He ate fresh fruits and vegetables and avoided processed foods, long before it was fashionable.

He wore all-cotton shirts.

He used a manual toothbrush.

He washed dishes by hand.

He wrote with a pencil.

He rode a bicycle to work.

He went barefoot a lot.

He had a wood-burning stove.

He never owned a computer.

He always took the steps.

Near the end of his life, someone put Bill on a ventilator. When he woke up and realized what was happening, he made them pull the plug.

Snow

Snow. Blinding snow, whipping snow, raging snow. Snow slicing sideways though the air like a frozen, pulverized river. Snow so heavy it bends trees and amputates limbs. Snow that disorients then buries animals. Howling snow, screeching snow, wailing snow. Snow that blots out the sun. Snow that fills in crevices and blankets lakes. Snow that freezes skin and calcifies fingers and toes. Snow that mummifies men. Drifts of snow, mounds of snow, mountains of snow. Biting snow, pounding snow, suffocating snow. Snow that blocks your advance and turns you back. Snow that falls for days and just keeps falling.

The Red Bridge

All the kids in my neighborhood crossed it on our way to school. Gently arched, the red bridge spanned a deep creek and made our journey through the woods safe and fun.

One summer evening, when I was 15, I met Lisa Roberts there. As kids, we'd crossed the bridge together many times, but we'd never been there alone. Now my throat felt tight. I felt dizzy.

Leaning over the railing, we watched fireflies flicker in the trees and listened to the restless murmur of the creek below. Then I turned to Lisa and kissed her, and she kissed me.

The List

The old man leaned forward in his chair and poked the glowing embers of the fire with a long stick.

He'd finally done it. He'd made a list of everything he'd ever done wrong. It had taken him weeks, but he wrote down everything he could remember—every sin, every slight, every regret.

With each entry, he paused to reflect on what he'd done and felt remorse and shame.

Now he dropped the pages into the fire, and they burst into flames. Just then, he began to think about the good things he'd done too—his kindnesses, his sacrifices, his generosity. They were all illuminated.

He sat back, weeping, as the paper turned to ash, and felt empty and full and at peace.

Fame

From the time she was a little girl, she had dreamed of being a famous singer and songwriter.

When the other kids were playing outside, she stayed in, listening to the most popular songs of the day and imagining herself on stage singing them or in a studio recording her own versions. She walked around her house with headphones on, singing. She sang in variety shows and competed in talent contests.

At 23, she won a Grammy for a song she had written and recorded about a girl in search of fame.

It was her first and only hit. In pursuing fame, she had forgotten to live and never learned that life, not fame, is the stuff of song.

The End of Ageism

When I was in my twenties, I started running on a bike trail along a river near my house. I ran fast, as I had all my life.

I said hello to other runners as they passed me. The other young runners, that is. Older runners didn't interest me. In fact, for some reason, they made me feel uneasy.

Every once in a while, I'd see this older man on the trail. I'd watch him jogging toward me. But as he drew near, I would lower my gaze. Close up, I never looked at him or even acknowledged him.

In my thirties, I still ran at a good clip but not quite as fast. I'd still see the old man from time to time. Now he was trotting. When he got close, I'd still avert my gaze.

When I hit 40, I dialed back on running and started jogging. My knees began to hurt. I still said hello to the younger runners, but some of them, especially the women, seemed not to notice me.

And I'd still see that old man. Now he was walking. When I passed by him, I still didn't look at him.

At 45, my hips began to hurt, and I began to walk more than jog. None of the other runners paid much attention to me anymore. I felt invisible to women.

One day, I spotted the old man in the distance again. He was walking with a cane now. As I got closer, I decided to look at his face. I noticed his eyes were brown, like mine.

The closer I got, the more familiar he seemed. When we were just a few feet apart, I realized he bore a remarkable resemblance to me. In fact, his face looked like an older version of my own.

"Hello," I said, stopping.

"Hello," he said, smiling.

The Giveaway

Barbara and George had been close since they dated in high school. Too close, some said. After all, George was a married man.

They got together for lunch a lot. Everyone had a hunch something was up.

"We're just friends," Barbara would say if anyone asked about her relationship with George.

They attended their 50-year high school class reunion. At dinner, George's wife sat to his right, and Barbara sat to his left.

When his wife went to the restroom, George leaned over and speared a cube of steak on Barbara's plate with his fork. She smiled.

Case closed.

Keeping it Real

Mickey Stanley belted out the last line of his band's most famous song, "Portland Forever." The crowd screamed it out with him, holding up lighters, their fists in the air.

He might be as old as the older ones in the crowd and old enough to be the father of the younger ones, but Mickey still had it.

"Good night!" he shouted as the crowd roared for an encore.

Mickey had now been the lead singer for Oregon for more than 30 years. The band had cut a dozen albums and toured extensively in the 80s and 90s, and Mickey had made a fortune.

In his 40s, he started producing music for others. In his early 50s, he was surprised when Oregon's songs began to enjoy a resurgence. After requests from fans both young and old and the promise of a new record contract, the band got back together.

Now they were on the road again, promoting a new album. They'd just finished a series of West Coast concerts and landed in Portland. A driver was waiting for Mickey at the airport. Rock and roll the second time around had it perks.

Mickey looked out the window on the way home. He smiled as he thought about the size of the crowd at the concert at Stanford the night before, how much he enjoyed partying with college students afterwards and how positive the media reviews were that morning.

The limo pulled into his driveway. The driver got out and pulled Mickey's suitcase out of the trunk.

"I can take it from here," he said, handing the driver a fifty.

Mickey's wife, Patti, was standing in the front doorway.

"Welcome home," she said, smiling.

Mickey wheeled his bag up the front walk and gave her a kiss.

"I missed you," he said, embracing her.

"I missed you too."

It was dinnertime, and Patti had made them hot dogs and french fries. As they sat down at the kitchen table, she filled their glasses with cold water from a plastic pitcher.

"So tell me about the tour," she said.

He had just begun telling her about the size of the crowds when the phone rang.

"Do you mind if I get that?" she asked.

"No, go ahead."

Mickey squirted ketchup on his plate, picked up a french fry and dipped it in.

"Sorry," said Patti a few minutes later. "That was Jane. She just got home from the hospital."

"How's she doing?"

"Pretty good. I baked her some cookies today. I'll take them over after dinner."

"That's nice."

"By the way," she said, "it's garbage night."

"Oh, yeah."

"And the grass is about a foot high, and it's supposed to rain tomorrow afternoon. Do you think you could cut it in the morning?"

"Sure."

"Now, what were you saying about the tour?"

A Little More Conversation

I walked into Starbucks, needing some hot coffee and hoping for some warm conversation.

A saxophone sounded like a man begging. A young woman at the counter rattled off an impossibly complex order to a young man who simply smiled and nodded.

The place was packed. Yet aside from the hissing espresso machine and the wailing sax, it was as quiet as a monastery. Everyone stared at their computer screens, most with wires dangling from their earbuds. No one said a word.

"Is this for here or to go?" asked the barista.

"To go," I said reluctantly.

Outside the Lines

On the first day of kindergarten, Becky's teacher, Ms. Williamson, handed out drawings of a teddy bear and told her students to color them.

"Try to stay inside the lines," she said.

The children grabbed their crayons and got to work. Most stayed safely within the lines. A few strayed a bit.

With Becky's teddy bear, though, every line was crossed—by a wide margin.

"Why did you do that?" Ms. Williamson asked.

"He's jumping around," Becky said.

Throughout grade school, Becky got F's in art. Much to her teachers' dismay, she never stayed inside the lines.

Today Becky teaches quantum physics at MIT.

Perfect to a Fault

Michael Chapman set the template on his desktop computer to five copies and pressed print. He stepped over to the printer, pulled off the five sheets of paper and returned to his desk.

He surveyed the writing instruments sticking out of a coffee mug on his desk, poked at a few of them and plucked out a black one with a thin, felt tip. Pulling off the cap, he signed his name on the first copy of the letter. Then he slid that copy aside and signed the second. Then the third, fourth and fifth.

He spread all five copies out on the desk and scanned his signatures. One stood out as most pleasing to his eye. He slid that one aside, collected the other four and inserted them into the paper shredder next to his desk.

For Michael Chapman, this was efficient. Sometimes he signed 10 or 15 copies of a letter before selecting one he felt was just right.

Of course, he knew it would be faster and easier to print and sign a single copy. But how could he be sure his signature would be perfect? Any letter which bore his name had to look its best. It was, after all, a reflection of him.

Michael had always been a perfectionist. As a boy, he would make his bed as soon as he got up in the morning.

Before he would fall asleep, he would lay out his clothes for school the next day, careful to coordinate the patterns and colors of his shirt, pants and even socks. His hair was always neatly combed, and his pencils were always sharp.

Striving for perfection served him well. When he was just 10, he made it to the finals in the national spelling bee in Washington, DC. He earned straight A's from kindergarten through college. His peerless GPA got him interviews with all the biggest accounting firms. When his classmates in college were still lining up interviews senior year, Michael landed a job with the prestigious CY.

At CY, he tackled every assignment with vigor. No one was more thorough or precise. He often went beyond the scope of his projects to offer his clients advice on ways to cut costs and increase profits. He gained a reputation as "a big thinker who sweats the details." When he was still in his mid-20s, the executives at CY had tagged Michael as partner material.

But by the time he turned 30, his fortunes had begun to change. His clients appreciated the quality of his work, but more and more they complained about his turnaround time.

One morning, his boss called Michael to his office.

"Good morning, Jim. You wanted to see me?"

"Yes, Michael," said Jim, sitting behind his desk. "Please have a seat."

Michael sat down. He had never had a high regard for Jim because his clothes were often mismatched. Today he was wearing a striped shirt and a striped tie. The stripes on his shirt were vertical. The stripes on his tie were horizontal. *He looks Cubist*, Michael thought.

"Michael, let me get straight to the point. You can't keep missing deadlines. I'll give you one more chance, but if you're late again—"

"I won't be late again," Michael said.

A simpleton and a Cubist, Michael thought as he walked out.

Two days later, Michael owed a client a recommendation on a tax-saving plan. It was a complex project. He had done weeks of research, including consulting with CY's tax attorneys, and identified several different strategic options.

Although he was leaning toward one of those options, Michael didn't feel he had worked through the implications sufficiently to make a strong recommendation to his client.

His proposal was due by the close of business that day. He thought about asking for an extension, but he knew what Jim would say—and what he would do. For Michael, being let go was simply out of the question.

Yet he was unwilling to advance a recommendation until he'd vetted it and could stand fully behind it.

There was only one thing to do. He sat down at his computer and composed a letter to Jim.

I hereby resign from CY.

Sincerely,

Michael Chapman

Then he set his template for five copies and pressed print.

Resolution

"So are you making any New Year's resolutions?"

"Nope."

"None at all?"

"Nope."

"Why?"

"Because I can never keep them and, when I don't, I get frustrated."

"I see."

"How about you?"

"Well, I've made one."

"What is it?"

"It's no big deal, really."

"Come on. No, wait. Let me guess."

"Okay."

"Lose weight."

"No."

"Eat healthier?"

"No."

"Exercise more?"

"No."

"New job?"

"No."

"Raise?"
"No."
"New car?"
"No."
"Bigger house?"
"No."
"Save money?"
"No."
"Travel?"
"No."
"Take up golf?"
"No."
"Learn a new language?"
"No."
"I give up. What is it?"
"To be more content with what I have."

The Puzzle

He had less than an hour to go when his Audi A6 began to shake and sputter. His engine stopped so abruptly that he didn't even have time to steer his car off the road.

It was a country road. Not many cars passed through there. But it would be dark soon, so he pushed his emergency flashers button, just in case.

Would AAA send someone all the way out here? He picked up his cell phone. *No service. Damn.*

He sat there, hoping someone would come along, but no one did. He opened his glovebox and looked for a map but found none.

This trip had seemed like such a good idea. Lord knows he needed the break. After years of constant stress and nearly non-stop travel, he was worn out. It was his wife who, out of worry for his well-being, had suggested he get away for a weekend up in White Mountain National Forest in New Hampshire. She even found a cabin for him there.

And now, so close to his destination, his car breaks down in the middle of nowhere. Maybe this trip wasn't such a good idea after all, he thought.

Should he take a chance on someone coming by or go find help? His eyes scanned the thick woods on both sides of the road, and he imagined the beasts living there. This is crazy, he thought. He opened the glove box again, reached in and grabbed a small flashlight. He got out, stuffed the flashlight in his pants pocket and started walking down the dusty road.

★

As a young man, Tom Adams knew exactly what he wanted: a beautiful wife, two kids and a high-powered, great-paying job. With these, he would be happy, he told himself. With these, his life would be complete.

Right out of college, he got an entry-level job in marketing at the headquarters of a fast-growing restaurant chain based in Connecticut. He hit the ground running, taking on every assignment and asking for more.

"CEO material," Tom's boss told his boss.

Soon, Tom was spending two days a week with his advertising agency in New York. Tom had a knack for advertising, and he helped the agency come up with a great new campaign and sell it to his management. Sales shot up as soon as the new ads hit, and Tom got the credit. By 32, he was chief marketing officer and, by 40, CEO.

When Tom was 28, at a party in New York, he met Ashley, the most beautiful woman he had ever seen. He asked her to dinner, and they fell in love. A year later, they were married.

Tom and Ashley moved into a pricey brownstone in Manhattan. They both had busy careers, and they were in no hurry to start a family. By their mid-30s, though, they were ready, and Ashley gave birth to Emily. Two years later, Josh was born, and the family moved into a small mansion in Greenwich.

And now, 300 miles away from home, Tom was walking alone down a dusty country road. He was the CEO of a major company, a multimillionaire, husband to a beautiful woman and father to two terrific children. According to his longtime dream, he should be happy, his life complete. But the more he had realized his dream, the more unhappy and empty he felt and the less certain he was about what would really make him happy.

★

When he had begun walking, there were woods along both sides of the road. The tall trees blocked the light, making it seem darker than it really was.

But now the trees began to thin, revealing open fields and pastures and the sun, not quite set, in the distance. The early evening air was warm and smelled like hay. About a mile up the road, he came to a wide gravel path, which led to a farm house. With no other house in sight, Tom stepped onto the gravel and made his way toward the house.

It was an old, wooden house, white with red shutters and a black weather vane on the roof. He walked up a stone path, stepped onto the blue-gray porch and knocked on the frame of the screen door.

A dog started barking, and he heard footsteps and voices inside. The door opened. There stood a sturdy, plain, pleasant-looking woman. She was flanked by a little boy and a little girl. A collie squeezed in front, barking non-stop.

"May I help you?" she said through the screen.

"I'm sorry to bother you," Tom said. "My name is Tom Adams. My car broke down about a mile down the road, and I can't get any cell service. I was wondering if I could use your phone to call triple A."

"Of course," she said, opening the screen door. "Please come in."

She reached down for the dog.

"Queenie! Stop! It's okay," she said.

Queenie stopped barking and looked up at Tom, wagging her tail.

"My name is Jessica," the woman said. "And these are my children, Emma and Jacob."

"I'm pleased to meet you," Tom said, shaking Jessica's hand and nodding at the kids.

"And I'm Matt," said a big, broad man stepping into the entryway.

"My husband," said Jessica, smiling.

"Pleased to meet you, Matt," said Tom, extending his hand. "Thank you for letting me use your phone."

"No problem," Matt said. "Right this way."

Tom followed him, with Jessica and the kids close behind and Queenie sniffing at his leg. They all walked into a large room. The walls were a warm shade of yellow. Several lamps filled the room with soft light. The sweet aroma of hot cocoa reminded Tom of his childhood. In the middle of the room stood a wooden table with four chairs. Hundreds of tiny puzzle pieces lay spread across the tabletop.

"We were just doing a puzzle," Jessica said.

"How fun," Tom said, remembering doing puzzles as a kid.

"Here you go, Tom," said Matt, pointing toward a telephone on an end table next to an overstuffed armchair.

The phone had a black, coiled cord. Tom hadn't seen a phone with a cord in years.

"Thank you," he said.

He grabbed his wallet, took out his AAA card and dialed the toll-free number. In the meantime, Matt, Jessica and the kids sat down at the table and resumed working on the puzzle.

Tom talked with AAA, then hung up.

"They said they'd be out in about an hour," he said.

"I'll be glad to give you a lift back to your car," Matt said.

"That'd be great."

"Do you like doing puzzles, Tom?" Jessica asked.

"I used to love puzzles," he said. "I haven't done one in a long time."

"Pull up a chair and join us," Matt said.

"Jacob," Jessica said, "please go get Mr. Adams a chair from the kitchen."

The boy got up and came back with a wooden chair.

"Here you go, Mr. Adams."

"Thank you, Jacob."

Jacob scooted his own chair over to make room for Tom.

"Would you like something to drink?" Jessica asked.

"I'd love some of that hot cocoa, if you have any extra."

"Sure do," she said. "I'll be right back."

"We'll take off in about 45 minutes," Matt said. "In the meantime, this is one tough puzzle, and we could sure use your help."

Tom looked down. The frame of the puzzle had been assembled. Tiny puzzle pieces were scattered all around, and there were a few small clusters inside the frame. But the lid to the puzzle box was nowhere to be seen, and without that, Tom couldn't tell what image they were trying to recreate.

When Jessica came back into the room, she could see Tom's eyes scanning the puzzle pieces.

"It's a farmhouse," she said, setting Tom's mug of hot cocoa down in front of him. "Like ours."

"See?" Emma said, pointing at a small collection of pieces toward the bottom of the frame. "This is a chicken."

"I see," Tom said, smiling.

Sipping his cocoa, Tom looked around the table, searching for pieces that might fit just inside the frame. He spotted one that appeared to be just the right color and shape, picked it up and slid it into place.

"You're good at this, Mr. Adams!" Emma said.

"Well, thank you, Emma. I used to love doing puzzles when I was your age."

"When you were 10?" she asked.

"Yes, when I was 10," he said. "That's funny. I have a daughter just your age."

"You do?" asked Emma.

"Yes. Her name is Emily. And I have a son named Josh. He's eight."

"That's how old I am!" Jacob said.

"Small world," Matt said.

Tom told them about Ashley and his kids, where they lived and where he was heading for the weekend.

"That's God's country," Matt said. "If you don't mind me asking, what brings you all the way up here?"

Tom didn't want to get into his troubles. He simply said he needed a break.

"I see," Matt said, asking no other questions.

Tom noticed how quiet it was. At home, he had grown used to the sound of a TV. But there was no TV in this room. Everyone spoke in low tones, focusing on doing the puzzle, and Queenie was now asleep. Tom had almost forgotten such calm was even possible.

But he remembered a time in his life that was calm, like this, when he was a boy. He remembered doing puzzles with his family too. They would gather around the kitchen table. Thinking of that table reminded him of his dad making pancakes after church on Sunday mornings. Tom loved those pancakes and, even more, those Sunday mornings with his family.

Now he spent his Sundays either at the office or on a plane heading to a meeting on Monday morning. He hadn't had breakfast with his family in years. And in that moment, it occurred to Tom that he had never made pancakes for his kids.

"Well, I guess we'd better get going," Matt said.

"Oh, yes," Tom said, as if awakening from a dream.

He got up and said goodbye to Jessica and the kids and patted Queenie on the head. He followed Matt outside, and they climbed into his pickup. When they got to Tom's car, a AAA tow truck was just arriving.

"I'll be okay now," Tom said, shaking Matt's hand. "Thank you for everything."

He pulled out his wallet and handed him a twenty.

"Keep it," Matt said. "Thanks for your help with the puzzle. Good luck this weekend."

The AAA driver, named Bob, was also a mechanic. He had Tom hold his flashlight as he checked under the hood.

"Here's your problem," Bob said. "Bad spark plugs."

He retrieved a cardboard box from his truck and replaced the plugs.

"Give it a try now."

Tom got in, and the engine started right away.

Bob closed the hood.

"You know where you're heading now?" Bob asked.

"Yes, I'll be fine."

"Okay, then. Have a good weekend."

"Thank you."

Tom watched the truck pull away. He looked at the clock in his car. It was a little after 10. He figured he was 45 minutes away from his cabin.

He thought about the prospect of spending the weekend there alone. He thought about the farmhouse family, so happy and content to be working together on that puzzle. He thought about his wife and kids at home.

Then he remembered his dream, and he realized that what he had wanted for so long was no longer what he really wanted and that what he wanted more than anything was to make pancakes for his family on a Sunday morning.

He turned his car around and started driving, knowing he'd make it home in time for breakfast.

Another Chance

I woke up. I was lying on my back, looking up at sunlight streaming through a hole high above.

I sat up and looked around. Others were waking up too. Some were walking around.

I stood up. I was in a cave, with solid walls all around. The only opening, it seemed, was the hole far above.

I looked at the faces of the others. They were the people who, throughout my life, had been my fiercest rivals.

And now here we were, trapped, with only one way out and, then, only if we could work together to manage our escape.

Mother Earth

"I don't think I can do this, George," Jane said with tears in her eyes.

"Do what?" he asked, taking her hands in his.

"Go on," she said. "I know we agreed, but I want to go home."

She buried her head in his chest and began sobbing.

"It's okay," he said. "I want to go home too."

"You do?" she asked, looking up into his face.

"Yeah," he said. "I miss the Earth already. I'll go talk to the captain."

★

They had signed up for this adventure knowing their children and grandchildren would be born in space. They would all be pioneers. The idea seemed so bold and exciting.

But now, just two days into their journey, watching the Earth shrink in the distance, they wanted only to feel the soft grass beneath their feet.

★

The ship was equipped with six escape pods, enough for the 10 passengers, the captain and her first mate. Two people could fit in each pod. Each had one small but powerful rocket booster and two auxiliary boosters. Each pod contained rations to last 30 days.

The idea was to give anyone who might need to use an escape pod the opportunity to make it to the closest planet, based on the premise that over time most, if not all, of the planets would be home to a space station.

★

"You're kidding," Captain Collins said in disbelief.

"I wish we were," George said. "I'm sorry we have to make this request, but we simply can't go on."

"Are you sure? If you leave, there's no way you can rejoin us, you know."

"Yes, I'm sure—and we know."

"Well, then, I'll let the flight director know so his team can begin preparing for your return."

"Thank you. When do you think we can leave?"

"I'd like to consult with Luca on that and, of course, coordinate with the flight director. But I suspect you and Jane will be able to take off yet today or tomorrow."

"Thank you, Captain. I'll let Jane know. She'll be so relieved."

★

First Mate Luca Virginio gave George and Jane instructions on how to gently guide their pod toward Earth, using the auxiliary boosters.

"Houston will talk you thorough everything," he said. "In about 10 days, you should be nearing the Earth's atmosphere and be ready to fire your main rocket booster. It'll be a rough ride at first, but then it should be smooth sailing. They'll probably have you land in the Pacific, near California. A ship will be waiting, and you'll be home in no time."

★

They splashed down off the coast of San Diego and were picked up by divers from a ship dispatched from a nearby naval base.

An hour later, the ship docked at the base. George and Jane thanked the crew, took questions from a few reporters waiting on the dock and headed for a green space down by the coast.

Five years earlier, they had met in a park, walking across the grass on a sunny day. A year later, they got married and began talking about the idea of raising a family in space.

Now George and Jane took off their shoes and walked in the grass. It felt so good beneath their feet. It felt so good to be home.

Far from Earth, they had discovered it is much more than a planet, much more than a stepping stone across the solar system. They began to understand the Earth is their mother. In the stillness of space, she had called them home, and they had heeded her call.

Now they cried for the loss of the adventure they had left behind and laughed imagining the one that lay ahead.

Terms

Two old friends sat together in a cafe, drinking coffee. They got together too seldom these days, it seemed. Unlike the old days, when they were inseparable.

In those days, there was an ease about their togetherness. They had an understanding. Sometimes they talked about important things, sometimes not. It didn't matter. They were simply together, and that was enough.

Lately, though, there was an awkwardness and a tension when they met, as one began making demands of the other. He had always been the more powerful, but he had always been generous and gracious too. Now, though, he began talking about the terms of their relationship.

"You expect too much," he said, "and give too little."

His friend was surprised and hurt. She tried to turn the conversation back to their shared interests, but he'd heard enough. He got up and left.

Choose

John Anderson ran for President making only one campaign promise: to help the American people choose a new path and then, having chosen it, help make it a reality.

He also said he would do this in one term and vowed not to run for a second.

He ran as an independent. He knew his odds were long and, at first, the pundits dismissed him. But voters so disliked the major party candidates and were so disillusioned with politics as usual that a slim majority decided to give Anderson a chance.

In his Inaugural Address, President Anderson said, "We are one people and, together, we must make tough choices about the rightful role of government in our lives. The role of government has grown too large. We need to be clear about what's most important to us and what we're willing to sacrifice."

The next day, in an Oval Office address to the nation, the new President announced he would embark the following day on a 50-day listening tour, attending town hall meetings in every state.

He said he wanted to hear what people wanted their government to do for them at the national level. Based on that, he said he would create a list of priorities for the federal government and work with Congress to fund these priorities.

He also said he wouldn't hesitate to cut programs that didn't make the list. In fact, as a sign he was serious, even before deciding *what* to cut, he pledged to reduce federal government spending by five percent a year over each of the next four years.

"I'm going into this with both eyes open," he said. "I know there's not a special interest out there that's not going to be upset. But there is a time to put aside our partisan interests, and make sacrifices, for the common good. That time is now."

★

The next 50 days were madness. Everyone had a special interest to protect, and everyone advocated and tried to rally support for that interest. Nearly everyone argued for more, not less, government spending. Nobody talked about what they were willing to cut.

But over the course of 50 days, some themes began to emerge. It became clear that most people wanted the federal government to protect them and ensure their basic rights, that they now considered health care one of those rights and that they agreed with the need to get government spending under control.

At the conclusion of his tour, President Anderson again addressed the nation from the Oval Office. His speech lasted less than two minutes.

"My fellow Americans, you have spoken, and I am listening. You've been clear that you want your government to protect you and your rights, provide free health care for all and cut spending. Next week, I'll submit my recommendations accordingly to Congress and begin working with Congress to *both* invest in these priorities *and* cut spending."

The President then did just as he said, working directly with both houses of Congress to fund the new national priorities and cut government spending by five percent in the coming year, mainly by trimming military expenses and so-called entitlement programs and closing corporate tax loopholes.

And he kept doing it over the remainder of his term. In the process, he made good on his sole campaign promise, and people's faith in government was restored.

Gratified, Anderson prepared to leave office. He chose not to run again, but his fellow Americans weren't finished choosing. A majority wrote him in and elected him for another four years.

Merry Christmas

I see him every morning, standing at the corner, holding a cardboard sign. The light there changes so fast that he usually makes it only to the first car stopped. I always hang back.

But I feel bad for him in his ragged clothes. As the temperature drops, I worry about him.

Lately he's been wearing a Santa hat. This morning, I pulled up to the light and rolled down my window.

"Merry Christmas, sir!" he said.

"Good morning," I said, handing him my winter coat.

"Thank you!" he said, flashing a gap-toothed smile.

"Merry Christmas," I said, pulling away.

Extremes

George Abbott was a man of extremes. To be more precise, he pushed the limits of everything and everyone, especially himself.

He worked harder than anyone. His company led its industry on every measure. He pushed his employees to achieve more every quarter. He acquired more wealth than just about anybody. His home was the largest in the city. He married four women, divorced them all and sired 10 children. He ate like a horse and weighed as much as a pig.

One night, George had a dream. He dreamed he was a pendant, suspended from a great pendulum by a thread. He had swung to one side as far as he could go. Any farther and the thread would snap. He knew he must stop and swing back or risk flying into the abyss.

The next day, George put both his company and his house up for sale. He instructed his attorney to divide his proceeds equally among his children and his ex-wives.

A few days later, he moved into a small apartment with no furniture, except for a mat. He began eating only one bowl of rice a day and drinking only water.

Sitting on his mat, George began each day in prayer. Day after day, he talked with no one and saw only those passing by his window. He had no computer or cell phone. He read no books and watched no television.

Instead, he simply sat and reflected on the excesses of his life. He wondered how his life had veered off to such an extreme.

Over many months, George grew frail. One morning, after prayer, he fell backward, too weak even to sit up. He looked up at the ceiling, which opened, revealing blue sky.

George watched as the clouds became smaller, and he realized he was falling. He fell for a long time. Then his fall slowed. Eventually, he stopped falling. Then he began rocking, gently rocking, back and forth, as if he were in a cradle, rocking slower and slower and slower until at last he was centered and still.

Gold

The 20-somethings playing volleyball on the beach spotted an old man coming toward them, slowly waving a metal detector back and forth above the sand.

As he got closer, they laughed at him. But he didn't seem to notice. He was focused on his device as he shuffled along.

A little later, he passed by again. This time, his device began beeping. He stopped, pulled a small shovel from his pocket, knelt down and started digging.

Bending down into the shallow hole he had dug, he reached in and struggled to pull something up. Again, the 20-somethings laughed. One of them, though, a young woman, went over to help.

He had found a large gold nugget. It sold for $1.2 million at auction. The old man split it with the young woman who had helped him.

Newsflash

Nikolas was waiting in the grocery check-out line when he spotted his neighbor, Emily, just ahead. She didn't see him, though, because she was typing on her phone.

He stopped at Starbucks on his way home. Waiting for his tea, he looked around. Everyone was staring at their screens. He felt invisible.

As he returned to his car, a young woman nearly walked right into him. She was texting and seemed oblivious to the cars circling the crowded parking lot.

When he got home, Nikolas sat down at his kitchen table and got to work, crafting and posting fake news stories.

Expert

"Keep your arms straight!" Steve yelled over the whine of the engine.

I braced myself and tried again, for the sixth time. But once again, the handle of the towrope flew out of my hands. I plowed into the water, face first.

"Again!" Steve barked as he steered the boat back around. "Tips out of the water! Lean back! Let the boat do the work!"

I really didn't care about all that stuff. I only wanted to impress my girlfriend.

But I'd had enough. I slipped off my skis and swam in.

"Why I don't drive, and you take a turn?"

"No way," Steve said. "I can't ski."

The Barker

Everyone knew what he was. He was the carnival barker, the man who shouted and raved about what lay in store for those discerning enough to appreciate the wondrous world just inside. For only a token, he promised, each of them could witness things few had ever seen.

In previous times, most had simply walked by him, dismissing him as a fraud or even a clown. But now many of them had grown tired of the smallness of their world, and they handed him their tokens and, smiling, he took them and said they were in for "a tremendous experience."

Trust

Jennifer Mattson was more than 20 years older than Josh Parker when she began to fall for him. She was 48. He was just 27.

It was not a physical thing at first, although he did stand out simply because he was older than all the other students in her freshman English class. He was also well dressed, unlike her other students, who wore sweatshirts and jeans. But the main thing that attracted Jennifer to Josh was his unique combination of self-confidence and vulnerability.

During the first class of the semester, as everyone introduced themselves, he said, "I'm Josh Parker. I'm 27, so I guess I'm the old man in this class."

Everyone laughed.

"Tell us a little about yourself, Josh," Jennifer said.

"Well, I went to work right after I graduated from high school," he said. "I have a good job. I'm selling commercial time for WBZ radio and making good money."

"What brings you here, Josh?" Jennifer asked.

"I know my future's going to be limited without a college education," he said. "So I've decided to go to school while I'm working. I know it's going to take me a while to get my degree, but I don't mind. When I'm a CEO one day, it'll be worth it."

Once again, everyone laughed.

It was that blend of humility and bravado that got Jennifer's attention.

At first, Josh wasn't a very good student. His grammar, spelling and overall writing skills needed a lot of work. He was behind most of the other students in the class, and Jennifer didn't want to slow them down by going over the basics with everyone. So she offered to tutor Josh.

"Thank you," he said, smiling. "I'd love that."

"Great," she said. "Can you stay after class once a week?"

"No, I can't. I'm sorry. I need to get back to work right after class. Can we make it some other time?"

They quickly concluded that, given their schedules, meeting during the day wasn't going to work.

"Well, I'd be glad to meet you at a restaurant or, if you like, host you at my house," Jennifer said.

As soon as she mentioned her house, she felt uneasy. Might her offer seem inappropriate?

"I doubt we could get the privacy we need in a restaurant," Josh said. "I'd be glad to come to your place."

Josh said this with such earnestness, even innocence, that Jennifer said, "Okay. How about this Friday evening?"

"That would be great. Where do you live?"

★

Josh wasn't married, and Jennifer had been divorced for nearly five years. She didn't date much, and so the idea of having a man in her house was a big deal, even if it was a student.

Housekeeping wasn't one of Jennifer's strengths, even though there was no one else to clean up after since the kids had moved out. Knowing Josh would be coming over on Friday, she spent hours that week cleaning every room on the first floor.

She also got her hair cut and colored and her nails done.

★

Josh arrived at 7:00, right on time. He was wearing jeans, a black golf shirt and brown suede shoes.

"Hello, Josh. Thanks for coming over."

"Good evening, Professor. Thanks for hosting me."

Stepping inside and looking around, he said, "You have a beautiful home."

"Why, thank you, Josh. May I offer you something to drink?"

"No, thanks. I just had dinner."

"Okay. I thought we could work in the dining room. That's where I usually do my work. There's plenty of space there."

"Sounds good, Professor. Lead the way."

"Right this way," she said.

She started to walk ahead of him, then stopped and turned around.

"Josh, I want you to know it's okay to call me Jennifer, at least when we're not in class," she said.

"Okay, Jennifer."

Hearing him say her first name gave her a warm feeling inside and made her ears tingle.

As they sat down at the dining room table, she got a whiff of his cologne. It smelled earthy. She felt her heart beat a little faster.

He took some papers out of a black folder and laid them on the table.

"I had some questions on some of your edits and comments on these assignments," he said. "I thought we might start there."

"Certainly," she said.

He slid the thin stack of papers over to her. She went through the assignments one by one, explaining each of her edits and comments. Josh listened closely.

He then asked if he could share a draft of his latest assignment for her input before he finished it.

"That would be wonderful," she said.

"Thank you, Jennifer."

Again, she felt warm inside when he said her name.

He slid his paper over to her. She noticed the sinewy muscles in his forearm. She slipped her glasses back on and began to read it.

As she read, she could feel his eyes upon her. She looked up. He was indeed looking at her. Instead of looking away, though, he just smiled. She noticed how straight and white his teeth were.

She made notes on his paper for about 15 minutes.

"All right, Josh. I've got some comments and suggestions for you. But let me say first that this is a very good start."

"Thanks. And let me say I really appreciate how positive and constructive you are. I wish more of my teachers were like you."

Now her whole body was tingling.

She scooted her chair closer to his and slid his paper over until it was almost in front of him. He scooted his chair toward hers. Now only a leg of the table separated them.

She went over her comments slowly. After most of them, Josh said, "Got it." But after some, he said, "I'm not sure I understand." That vulnerability again. She was only too glad to explain further.

When they were finished with that assignment, he thanked her and put all his papers back in his folder.

"Anything else I can help you with?" she asked.

"No, I think that'll do it."

"May I offer you anything before you go?"

Hmmm, she thought. *That didn't sound right.*

"No, thanks," he said. "I've taken enough of your time. I'm sure you have things to do on a Friday night."

I wish, she thought.

"And I'm sure you have things to do too," she said.

"Not really," he said. "It's a quiet night for me."

"Me too."

"Well, it's really quiet in your house. Isn't anybody else home?"

"No. I live alone."

"Oh," he said, his eyes widening, as if he was realizing this for the first time.

He got up, and she got up too.

"Josh, I really appreciate the extra effort you're making in our class," she said, walking him to the front door.

"And I really appreciate the time you've spent with me this evening, Jennifer."

"Anytime."

"Really? I might take you up on that."

"I hope you do."

She opened the door. Before he stepped out, Josh turned to Jennifer and gave her a hug. His body was lean and firm. It felt so good to her.

He loosened his embrace and said good night.

"Good night," she said. "I'll see you in class on Monday."

She watched him walk away and wished she could have held him a little longer.

★

The next morning, Jennifer went to the gym to work out. Afterwards, she stopped at the market for groceries. She then went home to grade papers and get ready for her classes in the coming week.

Of course, that made her think of Josh. Sitting at her dining room table, she closed her eyes and took a deep breath through her nostrils. She could still detect a trace of his cologne in the air.

It was after five. She was hungry but not in the mood to make dinner, so she went out to a favorite Italian restaurant nearby. It was a warm and pleasant evening, and she sat on the patio. Since her divorce, she had learned to dine alone without feeling self-conscious, though she never learned to like it.

She spotted a middle-aged man and a younger woman a couple of tables over. They were having drinks. He was laughing and doing most of the talking. He kept leaning in, though she sat back, squirming a bit in her chair.

At one point, he reached across the table and rested his hand near her plate, as if he expected her to take it. Instead, she slid further back in her chair, looking uneasy. He said something and laughed. She looked surprised. She got up and headed toward the bathroom. He sat back in his chair, looking unhappy, and motioned to the waitress for the check. As soon as the young woman returned, he got up, and they left.

The next day, Jennifer got a call from her daughter Sarah. She often called on Sundays just to catch up. Sarah said she was fine, but from her anxious tone of voice, Jennifer sensed she really wasn't.

"Honey, is everything okay?" she asked.

"It's been a tough week, Mom."

Sarah told her that a few days earlier, she had to file a complaint with HR because her manager had begun coming on to her.

"At first, I didn't believe it," she said. "I mean he was such a great boss. He really helped me, and I trusted him. But when he began to flirt, I knew I couldn't work with him because I could no longer trust him."

They talked for a while longer. Jennifer thanked Sarah for sharing what had happened and told her she was proud of how she had handled it.

"Thanks, Mom," she said. "Sometimes it's hard to know who to trust. I'm glad I always have you."

★

The next day, when Josh walked in the classroom, he smiled at Jennifer and nodded, and she smiled at him.

He hung back after class.

"Thank you again for helping me last Friday," he said.

"It was my pleasure."

"I was wondering if we might do it again this Friday—if you're free, of course."

She looked at him, as if for the first time. She pretended she didn't know his name, only that he was one of her new students. She tried to put aside her feelings for him and see him as he was: a young man trying to get his college degree and depending on her to develop skills he would need to succeed in life.

Then she remembered the young woman in the restaurant, and she thought about Sarah.

"Josh," she said, "I wish I could, but I can't. I really want to help you. I'm happy to help you. But from now on, it has to be either here in the classroom or in my office. I hope you understand."

"Of course I do," he said, looking a little relieved.

They met several more times that semester in Jennifer's office, always with her door open. She always came prepared with helpful comments and suggestions on his writing. He listened carefully and continued to improve.

Josh earned a B in the class. It took him seven more years to get his undergraduate degree. During that time, he got married and took a new job. At 40, he became a CEO.

Kronberg

A young man, walking along a well-worn path through an old-growth forest, came upon an older man using a walking stick just ahead.

"Hello," said the younger man, careful not to startle him.

"Hello," the older man said with a smile.

"Heading to Kronberg?" the younger man asked.

"Yes. You?"

"Yes."

"What brings you there?" the older man asked.

"I've heard it's a beautiful town, but I haven't been there. I want to check it out."

"I see."

"How about you? Have you been to Kronberg?"

"Many times. I walk there nearly every day."

"What's it like?"

"I don't know. I always stop at the end of this trail and go back home."

Watercolors

"I'm sorry," the doctor said to the young couple sitting in the corner of the hospital room. "Sarah is gone. We did everything we could."

Karen put her head in her hands and let out an awful moan. David wrapped his arms around her. He looked up at the doctor and nodded, as if to dismiss him. Saying nothing more, the doctor slipped out.

The two of them sat there, holding one another and crying for a long time before David got up and asked the nurse if they could see their daughter again.

★

As a girl, Karen loved to paint with watercolors. Her mother gave her a set of watercolor paints for her fourth birthday. Karen loved dipping her brush in a cup of water, wiping it across the little cakes of vibrant colors and creating images on sheets of white paper.

At first, her work was wild, a flurry of bold and colorful brushstrokes. But before long, recognizable objects began to emerge: a tree, a house, the sun.

By six, Karen was painting basic landscapes. By seven, she was painting the sea. She had never been to the ocean. But her parents had a coffee table book which featured a spectacular collection of photographs of the natural world. Karen used to study the pictures in that book for hours.

One day, she brought the book into her bedroom, where she now painted with an easel. She propped it open to a favorite photo: a two-page, panoramic shot of the Atlantic Ocean taken from the docks of a fishing town in New England.

She painted that scene over and over, improving it each time. She even began blending colors to get just the right shades for a wooden boat, a swooping seagull and the glint of noonday sun on the waves.

Recognizing her talent and her promise, Karen's parents enrolled her in art school at age eight. Karen blossomed, painting all kinds of things.

She was mesmerized by things. She could sit and gaze at the horizon or a hillside of wildflowers for hours. To Karen, such things seemed like natural objects of art.

She learned to use acrylics, pastels and oil paints, but she always came back to watercolors.

"They just feel right," she said.

When Karen was 14, several of her paintings were featured in a local art exhibition. Afterwards, a woman contacted her mother to ask if she could buy one. Her mother had Karen follow up with the woman directly, and she sold her first painting for $50. The young artist was ecstatic.

Karen kept painting all through high school, and her paintings began to be featured in regional art shows. The broader exposure led to even more interest in her work, and she began selling many of the paintings she exhibited.

Some people asked Karen to do portraits, but she demurred. “People move too much,” she said.

Buoyed by the growing interest in her work and the prospect of a steady income from painting, Karen decided not to go to college but instead open her own art studio. It was there, during an open house one Friday evening, she met David.

They fell in love and were married a year later. Two years after that, Sarah was born. She lived three days.

★

After Sarah died, Karen felt lost. She tried to paint but couldn't. Nothing seemed to interest her anymore. Not trees or mountains or even the sea.

One day, she decided to take a walk at a nearby park. She had walked there many times. Sometimes she even brought her easel and painted there.

Now she walked along a path through the woods. Yet even though she was immersed in nature, she seemed oblivious to it.

Near the end of the trail was a large jungle gym. About A dozen children were climbing on it, sliding down the slide and swinging on the swings, their mothers hovering nearby.

At first, the children made Karen think of Sarah, and she was tempted to keep walking. But she was tired and sat down on a bench to rest.

She watched the children at play. She looked at their faces and saw how joyful they looked.

Karen closed her eyes. In her mind, she could see Sarah's face. Not as it was in her brief time on earth, but how it was just then. She was smiling, and her deep blue eyes were open. Looking into them, Karen felt so close to her, as if they were one, not just in that moment but for all time.

She opened her eyes and saw the happy faces of children and mothers. She saw trees and clouds too. But now these things were just a backdrop to the people before her.

Karen drove home. She found a photograph David had taken of Sarah as a newborn. Her eyes were open, and she had a faint smile on her face, and Karen remembered her daughter looking up at her at that moment.

She went into their second bedroom, which served as her art studio. She clipped the photograph to her easel and, in watercolors, began recreating the face of her daughter.

★

From then on, Karen painted every day—but only people, not things.

In time, she and David had three more children. They filled her life with joy, and she painted many portraits of them.

Over the years, Karen's paintings became popular all over the world. People said the faces of the people in her paintings spoke to them.

Karen considered painting with oil or acrylics, but she stayed with watercolors. With every face she painted, she thought of Sarah. Sometimes this made her cry, and her tears would blend with her paint.

The Wall

There it stood, 30 feet tall, made of concrete and steel. It stretched in both directions as far as the eye could see. It was gray, of course, the color of despair.

They built it to keep the "bad guys" out. At least that's what they said. But the real message was clear: we don't want any of you here.

At first, a few tried to scale it, but it was no use. It was a well designed wall. No one got through.

Soon, they stopped trying. But in the process, they also stopped wanting to get to the other side—or to leave their homeland at all.

Unable to find a better life elsewhere, they began improving their own society, calling on their own business people, scientists and artists. In less than a decade, they managed an astonishing turnaround. They captured the world's imagination, and people from everywhere went there to live, work and trade.

Except those who had built the wall. They were content to keep the new overachievers out and focus on themselves.

For a while, they continued to prosper. But as their population aged and shrank, they needed workers, and they put out a call for help.

But the people of the world ignored them. Most wanted nothing to do with a society which puts itself first and builds a wall to keep others out except when it needs them.

The sons and daughters of those who had built the wall began to feel trapped by it, and they tore it down. But it was too late. They had become ostracized, even as they had ostracized others.

In time, the descendants of the wall builders once again became part of the world. Not because ugly memories had faded but because they themselves at last remembered who they were.

Inside Out

The boy stepped up on the front porch and rang the bell. A woman opened the door.

"Good morning, Josh," she said.

"Can Jake come out?"

"He's in his room, playing video games. Would you like to join him?"

"No, thanks."

Josh walked to other friends' houses, but their moms and dads said they were inside too, most of them playing video games.

And so it went for much of Josh's childhood. While his friends played indoors, he played outdoors, wading through creeks, climbing trees and hiking in the woods.

This morning, now Secretary of the Interior, Josh announced a name change—to the Department of the Exterior.

Three Minutes

At Fairmont Grade School, every year in October, coaches of the A and B teams in basketball pick their players for the coming season. There is a sign-up sheet for C team players.

Once again, Bill Collier would be coaching the sixth grade C team. He had just picked up the sign-up sheet for his new players. That evening, he got a call from Frank Heatherton, whose son Jimmy had signed up for Bill's team.

"Hello, Frank. How are you?"

"I'm good, Bill. I'm calling about Jimmy. He's signed up for your basketball team this year."

"I saw that. I look forward to coaching him."

"And Jimmy can't wait to play for you. But there's something I need to make you aware of."

"What's that?"

"Jimmy has a heart condition."

"I'm sorry to hear that. Can he still play?"

"Well, that's the thing. His doctors say he can play sports, but if he does, he shouldn't exert himself for more than a few minutes at a time."

"I'm not sure I understand."

"I mean that Jimmy can play for you, but if you put him in, I'd like you to take him out after just a few minutes."

"Are you serious?"

"Yes."

"Are you sure this is safe for him?"

"Yeah, I'm sure. Jane and I have talked about it, and we're okay with it—as long as he doesn't play more than a few minutes at a time."

"Is Jimmy okay with that?"

"Bill, Jimmy loves basketball. He practices on our driveway all the time. He's a great shot. But he's never played on a basketball team. He's never played any organized sport. When he found out he could sign up for your C team, he was thrilled. He really wants to play—and, yes, he understands his boundaries."

"This is a very unusual situation, Frank."

Silence.

"And I realize it's a very unusual request," Bill added.

"I know it is, Bill, and if you decide it's not something you can accommodate, I'll understand. You're in charge. I'll just tell Jimmy basketball's not going to work for him this year."

Bill thought about it for a moment. He knew Jimmy. He was a friend of his son. He found it hard to imagine putting Jimmy or any player into a game so briefly, but if he wanted to play that bad, Bill didn't want to stand in his way.

"No, Frank. It's okay. I'll find a way to make it work."

"Thanks, Bill. Oh, there's one more thing."

"What's that?"

"Very few people know about Jimmy's heart condition. He's very self-conscious about it, as you might imagine. He doesn't want to be seen as weakling. Jane and I have told him it's okay, it's just the way he's made. But Jimmy insists on not telling anyone. So we would ask that you not tell anyone about Jimmy's heart condition. Okay?"

"Sure, Frank. I understand. I won't say a word."

"Great. Well, thanks, Bill. I'll tell Jimmy we've talked, and you'll find a way to let him play. I know he'll be delighted."

As soon as Bill hung up, questions began to fill his head. *How can I put Jimmy in for such a short time without disrupting the game? Won't people wonder what's wrong with him? What if I keep him in too long and his heart fails?*

But Bill knew he had just told Frank yes and that, by now, he was probably telling Jimmy he was going to play basketball this year and that Jimmy was probably whooping and pumping his fists in the air.

He was just going to have to figure out a way to make this work.

★

On the first day of practice, Bill gathered his 15 players together and had them sit on the bleachers.

After having each of the boys introduce himself, he handed out their practice schedule and shared his expectations for the upcoming season.

Then he told the boys he was going to try something new this year.

"For all of our games this season," he said, "I'm going to put each of you in for three minutes at a time."

The boys stared at him, then looked around at each other. A few laughed.

"What?" one asked.

"It's a new approach," Bill explained. "I have a theory that we can actually play better and score *more* points if I change players every three minutes."

"You're kidding," said one of the boys.

"No, I'm serious. Think about it. If I told you that you're going into a game for only three minutes, wouldn't you make the most of those three minutes? Wouldn't you figure out how you can best get the ball to the basket or best prevent the other team from scoring? That would be your total focus because you would know that, in three minutes, you'll be back on the bench."

The boys grumbled and rolled their eyes.

"I know it sounds like a stretch, guys. But I'm asking you to try it. If it doesn't work, we'll try something else. But I think it's going to work. Not only that, I think you're really going to like it."

★

Just before the first game of the season, Bill sent a note to the parents of his players, telling them about his new approach and why he felt it was going to be good for the team and each of the boys. He got calls from a few parents, complaining that their sons wouldn't get enough playing time. But Bill assured them that now every player would actually play a little more than he otherwise would. This helped, though not all the parents were buying in.

Bill also called the coaches of the other teams to give them a heads-up. None of them liked Bill's new system. One called it crazy. But they all respected Bill and gave him a pass.

In the first game that season, Bill started Jimmy at guard. Less than a minute into the game, Jimmy scored the team's first two points. He was ecstatic. Two minutes later, Bill took Jimmy and his other four players out, and another five boys took their places.

At first, swapping players this way was awkward and disruptive. But by the second half, both Bill's team and the opposing team had grown used to it.

And it worked well for Bill's team. They ending up winning that game by 19 points. What Bill had predicted came true: each of his players, knowing he would be in for only three minutes at a time, made the most of that time. Each of them played up and, as a result, the whole team played up too.

Bill's team finished with an 18-2 record, first in the league. It was the best performance of any team Bill had ever coached.

Everyone was happy but most of all Jimmy, who was the team's leading scorer. Bill selected him as MVP.

Welcome

The snow whipped at his eyes, nearly blinding him. Frostbitten and exhausted, he stood frozen, unsure which way to go and unable to take another step.

He'd been walking for nearly two days. That's when the blizzard hit and he got separated from his countrymen. That's when he got lost.

He was just about to give up when, in the distance, he saw a small light. What was its source? Could he make it there? He wasn't sure, but he knew he had to try. And so he reached deep, summoning the last trace of his strength, and headed toward the light.

As he inched closer, he could see the light was coming from the tiny window of a stone hut. His heart leapt.

Again and again, he stumbled in the deep snow, but he pressed on until he at last reached the hut. He tried to lift his hand to strike the wooden door but was too weak. All he could do was fall against it.

A few moments later, someone pulled it open. Inside, a man wearing a maroon robe gathered the stranger in as he collapsed in his arms. He carried him across the stone floor and gently placed him on a rug before a roaring fire. Then he covered him with a wool blanket and tucked a pillow under his head.

Lying on his back, delirious from the cold and now the sudden warmth, the stranger looked up into the wide, dark face of his host.

"Heb-bar kaa-su-shu," the man said softly, smiling.

The stranger did not know Tibetan, but he knew the sound of welcome.

Marketing Whiz

In the summer, the kids in TJ's neighborhood sold lemonade at the end of their driveways for a nickel a cup.

TJ took a different approach. He sold various flavors of Kool-Aid in plastic gallon jugs to workers building houses nearby. He showed up at their construction sites just before noon on dog days and charged $2 a gallon.

At summer's end, when the other kids were counting their coins, TJ opened a savings account and deposited more than $500, his proceeds after paying his mom for the packets of Kool-Aid.

Today TJ makes $500 an hour as a marketing consultant.

Berries

As boys, he and his brother spent a week every summer in northwestern Pennsylvania, where their father grew up. The summers are short there. By July, the blackberry, raspberry and blueberry bushes which cover the wooded hillsides are heavy with fruit.

Their father would take them into the woods to pick berries. When their bushels were full, they would leave the cool woods and hike back in the warm sunshine through meadows of green and gold, back to the old house, where Grandma would prepare bowls of mixed berries swimming in cream and sugar.

Those vacations were an adventure because, as boys, the brothers lived in the city, and there were no hills or meadows or berry bushes there.

Now they're grown men, and they live a thousand miles apart. Their lives are busy, and they seldom see each other anymore. Their grandmother is gone, and the old house in Pennsylvania was sold long ago.

But every year in July, they get together. They go to the local market and buy fresh berries. They bring them home, wash them and gently drop them into bowls. Then they pour cream over them and sprinkle them with sugar.

They sit down at the kitchen table, bring spoonfuls of berries to their lips and breathe them in. They open their mouths and close their eyes and let the sweetness and tartness of the berries dance on their tongues, and they go back to the hills of Pennsylvania, to their grandmother's house, to a slower and simpler time.

The Course of History

Anatoly Popov stood back from the machine, which was humming and blinking and shaking ever so slightly. It was running at full tilt now. All he needed to do was step inside, set the date and push a button. Then, at last, if all his calculations were correct and all his work was precise, he would be transported in time.

He was well aware of the enormity of his challenge and the length of his odds. But he was steadfast in his belief that he could do it and, even more fundamentally, that he should do it. He had devoted his life to science. He had mastered quantum mechanics and applied everything he knew in designing and building this machine. That is what made him confident it would work.

But what made him confident he should use it had nothing to do with science. He had a deep belief that the Revolution many years earlier had been ill-conceived and misguided and that, in it, lay the seeds of misery and destruction for untold millions in the years to come.

He had, therefore, dedicated his life to creating a machine that could transport him back to the eve of the Revolution, so he could help derail it and change the course of history.

Now his machine hummed at a fevered pitch. Anatoly set his jaw and stepped inside. He pressed a series of numbers on the keypad in the wall: 1-7-1916. Then he pushed a green button. Everything around him began spinning, and he became light-headed and passed out.

When he awoke, Anatoly was lying in a field. He sat up and looked around. In the distance, he saw a horse pulling a plow, which was being guided by a farmer. He stood up and walked over to the man, who told him where he was and confirmed it was July 1916.

It had worked! Anatoly was thrilled. He went into the city, found a place to stay and got to work lining up opposition to the idea of overthrowing the imperial government.

The following March, in the early hours of the first of two revolutions, Anatoly was arrested. That November, after the second revolution, Anatoly was sent to a labor camp in Siberia.

He died there 10 years later, dreaming about escaping, building a time machine and traveling back to change the course of history.

A Most Special Guest

They gathered in the town square, where every important public event took place. They talked excitedly with one another.

"I wonder what he looks like."

"I wonder what he'll be wearing."

"He's a prince! He'll be wearing a robe, of course."

"And riding a white horse."

"I've heard he's filthy rich."

"I just hope he's generous."

A commotion arose at the edge of the crowd. It was a beggar. How embarrassing, especially at such a long-awaited moment.

"They're like parasites."

The authorities rousted the man, easing the crowd, allowing everyone to prepare for the arrival of their most special guest.

Deadly Pride

Ethel had an irrational fear of her hair turning gray, yet she had an aversion to coloring it. She felt hair dye was dangerous.

So she went to the library and read about natural ways to keep hair from turning gray. She learned that certain nutritional supplements, especially vitamin K, might help. On the way home, she stopped at the drug store and bought a big bottle of vitamin K.

The recommended dose was one tablet a day. Now in her forties and haunted by the specter of gray hair, Ethel started taking three tablets a day and worked her way up to six.

At 50, Ethel died of a heart attack. Her doctor said it was caused by a blood clot.

She had an open casket at her visitation. People there commented on the youthful beauty of her dark hair.

Go Back

I started out intending to run five miles, but my knees were hurting, so I decided to run three.

Maybe I'm getting too old for this, I thought. It seemed like a good idea five years ago, when I retired. But now that I was back in shape, running five days a week, I was thinking about cutting back. A little too much wear and tear on my aging body.

But then the pain in my knees subsided. Not only that, but I began to feel stronger. I had more spring in my step.

That morning, I had decided to run in my neighborhood and the adjoining neighborhoods. There were just a few busy streets to cross. As I waited for a walk sign at an intersection, I noticed how few SUVs were on the road and, even stranger, how many minivans there were. *Maybe they're making a comeback.*

I crossed the street and ran on. Remarkably, my hips, which had also been bothering me lately, didn't hurt at all now. All of a sudden, I was feeling great. *Maybe I'll run five miles after all.*

As I ran through a nearby subdivision, I was surprised to see so many older cars. The houses seemed older too. I hadn't run there in a while. I didn't remember this subdivision being that much older than mine.

Even stranger, my body was now feeling very different. I felt stronger and lighter. I'd been running on the flats of my feet for years, but now I was running on my toes, like I did when I was young, and running faster than I had in years. I wondered if my attempts at cutting back on sugar were finally paying off.

I ran through the subdivision and waited for the light to change at another busy intersection. Now the minivans were gone, and there were a lot of station wagons whizzing by. *How retro. Maybe they're making a comeback too.*

I was approaching the high school my kids had attended years before. But as I got close, the buildings looked different. They were smaller than I remembered, and the brick was red, not yellow. As I ran past the entrance, the sign out front said "Fairfield High School." This was not my kids' school! It was mine.

Where was I? I stopped running and looked around. Now all the houses looked old, but most of them were in really good condition, the way I remembered them when I was a kid. I looked up at the street sign. I was on the corner of Mississippi Drive and Potomac Avenue, just two blocks from my house as a kid.

I spotted a familiar car parked on the street. It was a green 1965 Chevy Impala, just like the one our neighbor, Mr. Asher, used to drive. As I walked past it, I saw my reflection in the window. I could hardly believe my eyes. I was thin and young, with a full head of long, brown hair! I looked down. I was wearing white Converse tennis shoes, tube socks and red and white gym trunks, my high school colors. *What the hell was happening?*

I kept walking. A few minutes later, I was standing at the end of my old driveway. I looked up and saw my old house. It seemed so small. The garage door was up. I recognized my old Schwinn Varsity 10-speed bike inside.

I felt like I was losing my mind. *How could that possibly be my old bike? It was stolen when I was in college. How could this be my old house?*

I had to find out. I walked up the driveway and into the garage. It was a two-car garage, but we had only one car, and it was gone. I walked past my bike to the door that led into our house. It was open. I could see into the dining room through the wood-framed screen door. It was a warm day. I remembered we didn't have air conditioning when I was a kid. We kept the doors and windows open a lot.

I heard someone inside. *Dare I go in?* I grabbed the handle of the screen door and pulled it open. A spring on the hinge side of the door sounded like a cartoon character pulling a pig's tail.

"Patrick, is that you?" came a voice from inside. It was my mother. *But how could it be? She had died last year.*

I was standing in the dining room, just inside the door, when she peeked out from the kitchen.

"Oh, it's you," she said. "How was your run?"

It *was* my mother. She looked so young. I was stunned. I couldn't move.

"Well, how was your run?" she asked again, wiping her hands with a small towel. "Are you okay?"

"Yeah, Mom," I finally managed to say. "How are you?"

She laughed.

"I'm fine, Patrick. Same as I was an hour ago, when you left for your run."

"That's good," I said.

It was all I could muster. I walked through the dining room and into the kitchen. My mom was peeling potatoes at the sink. Her hair was dark, and her waist was thin. She glanced back at me and said, "Now go get your shower. Your dad will be home in less than an hour."

"Dad?"

"Yeah," she said. "We're going to eat as a family tonight."

I struggled to grasp what she was saying. *How could my father be home in less than an hour?* He'd been gone for nearly 10 years.

"Where are Doug and Beth?" I asked.

"Doug's at baseball practice," Mom said. "Beth's in her room, studying."

"Beth's in her room?"

"Yes, and don't you dare bother her. She's got a big math test tomorrow."

This was all far too weird. My little sister Beth, who was now 56 years old and a grandmother, was in her bedroom studying for a sixth grade math test?

I wasn't sure what to do. Part of me wanted to obey my mother and take a shower. Part of me wanted to go see Beth. Part of me wanted to wait to see my father, to talk with him again.

But a voice inside me was telling me to leave, to get out of there, to go back to my home—I mean where I live now. I thought of my wife, my children and my grandchildren. I knew I had to get back to them. And somehow I knew that if I didn't leave soon, if I became too attached to this place and time and these people, I might never be able to go back.

"Mom, I said, "I'll be right back."

"Where are you going?" she asked, turning around.

"To finish my run," I said. "I won't be long."

"Patrick, sometimes I just don't understand you," she said, shaking her head.

I stepped toward her, opened my arms and embraced her.

"I love you, Mom," I said, kissing her on the cheek.

"I love you too," she said. "What brought that on?"

I stood back from her and looked into her eyes.

"I didn't tell you that enough," I said. "I didn't tell Dad enough either. Will you tell him for me, please? When he gets home, will you tell him I love him?"

"Patrick, you're not making any sense. Why don't you tell him yourself?"

"I can't, Mom. I can't do that. Just tell him, please."

She shook her head again and smiled.

"Okay," she said. "I'll tell him."

"Thank you," I said. "Goodbye, Mom."

"Goodbye, Patrick."

I walked back through the dining room and out into the garage. I ran my hand across the hard leather seat of my old bike. I loved that bike. I was tempted to hop on and ride away. But I knew I had to return the same way I'd arrived, on foot.

I walked to the end of the driveway, took one last look at my old house and started running home.

Pink House

It was an old, two-story house, three stories if you count the stand-up attic. High on a corner lot, it caught your eye because it was pink.

They lived there together for 30 years. She tiptoed through the house and dusted twice a week. He cursed loudly, slammed doors and broke knick knacks. He drank too much, and he was a mean drunk. When he came home drunk, she hid from him.

He had no interest in painting his house pink, but she liked the color and asked him to do it.

And so he would take a week off of work in the summer. He would climb a ladder in the searing heat and sweat and scrape and sand and paint and drink only water.

When he was finished, he would go inside and take her hand. They would walk down the front steps, out onto the sidewalk and look up at his handiwork.

"Oh, I love our home," she would say, wrapping her chubby arm around his thin waist.

He would smile and cup his hands around his eyes to shield them from the sun and hide his tears.

Barefoot

When he was a boy, his mother couldn't see him when it was time to come home, but she knew he was wading in the creek behind their house.

She would call for him, but the rushing water drowned out her voice. She would have to go to the edge of their property and wave her arms to get his attention.

"Why are you always down here?" she would ask.

"I love the way the water feels on my feet."

When he grew up, he went to work for a shoe company. Now he's the CEO.

Most days, he works from home, so he can go barefoot.

Aidan's Way

"Come with us this morning," Emily said.

"No, you guys go ahead," Kaitlyn said.

"You never walk with us anymore," said Emma.

"She's weird," whispered Madison.

"I'll see you at school," said Kaitlyn.

Kaitlyn headed toward a field as her friends continued down the sidewalk, following a more far direct route to school.

Kaitlyn crossed the field and came to some woods. She followed a path through the trees. It had rained the night before, and a fresh, clean aroma arose from the earth. She crossed a wooden bridge over a creek. Birds sang sweetly in the trees.

This way is so much more interesting, she thought. No wonder Aidan loved it.

Just beyond the woods was a four-lane highway. Kaitlyn stopped at the intersection and waited for the walk sign. If only Aidan had paid closer attention.

Believe

"I've got to say that's a pretty wild story," he said.

"Well, it's true," she said.

"You're sure?"

"What do you mean? Why would I lie about something like that?"

"I don't know. It's just that it happened so long ago. Memories get fuzzy."

"There's nothing unclear in my mind."

"Was anybody else there when it happened?"

"No."

"Did you tell anybody?"

"No."

"Why?"

"I felt ashamed."

He sighed.

"You know if you talk about this, people are going to attack you."

"I know."

"It's bound to get ugly."

She closed her eyes, frowned and nodded.

"But I believe you," he said.

Who's Calling?

We had just bought a Victorian home in Connecticut. It was in our price range because it needed a lot of work—and a rumor the place was haunted.

I went downstairs to catch up on some reading. One of the previous owners had built a large, red phone booth with a chair and small desk inside. It even had one of those old-fashioned telephones on the wall, although the realtor said it was just for decoration.

I had just sat down and opened my book when the phone rang.

We put the house on the market the next morning.

The Meaning of Life

"Good morning, ladies and gentlemen," Professor Dumont intoned. "Welcome to transcendental metaphysics."

His 25 students, most of them sophomores, were barely awake. All of them were there to fulfill their philosophy requirement. None was excited to be there.

"You might be wondering what this class is about," the old man said in a cadence suggesting he'd done this many times before. "In this class, you will discover the meaning of life."

Snickers.

"What is so funny?" he asked.

No one said a word.

"Ladies and gentlemen, that was not a rhetorical question. Who can tell me what is so funny about what I said?"

A student raised her hand. Dumont looked at her and nodded.

"It sounds absurd," she said, prompting more snickers.

"Exactly," the old man said, clasping his hands together. "And why does the absurd sometimes make us laugh?"

These were the first of many questions Professor Dumont would pose to his students that semester. By the end of that first class, his students would begin posing questions of their own.

Soon, they began questioning everything. Their questions were thoughtful and incisive, and they didn't always lend themselves to easy answers. One question often led to another, and the students pursued the answers together, as if they were on a scavenger hunt. They went deeper and deeper, searching for one truth after another.

Finally, in the last class of the semester, one of the students reminded Dumont that he had said they would discover the meaning of life.

"But you already have," he said with a smile. "It is to question."

Flashpoint

Pete and I had been kayaking for about an hour in Glacier Bay, Alaska, when we spotted something in the distance. It looked like a shadow on the water. At first, I thought it was a boat. But then it disappeared—then reappeared. It was probably 200 yards away. Whatever it was, it was big.

"Holy crap!" Pete cried. "I think it's a whale!"

I felt my chest tighten. I felt dizzy. I had just learned to control my lifelong fear of water, and now it came rushing back. I had an overwhelming urge to get the hell out of this little boat and feel the earth beneath my feet.

I looked around to find our group. Once again, Pete and I had wandered off. We were 100 yards from the others. And we were all a mile from the small ship that all 14 of us called home that week.

"Pete, let's get back with the group," I said.

"No way," he said. "We're staying put. John said if we see a whale, we shouldn't move."

"Maybe it's not a whale."

"You're right!" Pete shouted. "It's not a whale. It's *three* whales!"

Sure enough, I now saw three whales in the distance, and they were heading our way.

Damn! Sometimes I hated it when Pete was right.

★

A week before, Pete and I had put our laptops away, kissed our families goodbye and set out for Alaska. It was July 2007.

I had known Pete for nearly 20 years. For much of that time, he had been asking me to take this trip with him. Pete had been to Alaska twice. He raved about it. His voice would get high-pitched, like a kid, when he told me about glaciers "calving icebergs," huge chunks of ice breaking off the end of glaciers and plummeting into the bay.

"They're as big as a school bus!" he would exclaim, stretching out his arms and thrusting his fingers into the air. "You're kayaking along and, all of a sudden, crack! The next thing you know, that ice hits the water, and the impact creates a huge wave. If you're too close, it'll swamp you and flip your boat. But if you're just far enough away, you can ride it. What a rush!"

Breathlessly, Pete told me about the time he dove off the side of a boat, without a wetsuit, into the frigid water below.

"It was a sunny day, but the water was 38 degrees," he said. "There was ice floating in it. Without a wetsuit, you've only got a few minutes to live. After a minute, your arms begin to freeze. So you can't jump out too far, and you have to swim fast."

Pete said when he hit the water, it was like being in another world.

"Everything is deep blue," he said. "You can't believe how cold that water is. At first, it stings like hell. Then you can't feel a thing. And you can't hear anything, except for the beating of your heart. Boomp, boomp. Boomp, boomp. Boomp, boomp," Pete murmured, thumping his chest.

Yet Pete kept diving. He forced himself to go deeper until he could go no farther. When he finally surfaced, he heard the cheers of the other passengers watching from the safety of the deck.

"I was out farther than I thought," he said.

When he realized just how far from the boat he was, Pete tried to swim hard. He was a strong swimmer. But now his arms felt like lead, and he struggled to lift them. Tiny icebergs bounced off his 250-pound body. He felt like he was in slow motion. By the time he got close to the boat, he could barely move, and he could no longer feel his arms.

"But our guide was watching everything," he said, smiling, "and he pulled me up on deck just in time. It was incredible!"

Of course, none of us believed him. Who would do something so crazy?

But Pete had proof: a photograph someone on the boat had taken of him in the water. He carried it, folded and tattered, in his wallet. Sure enough, there was Pete—a walrus of a man, mustache and all, his blanched, bare torso jutting out of the icy water, his right arm extended forward and up, his hand grasping another man's hand, his lips blue, his thinning hair glazed on his forehead, his eyes half-closed. He was probably seconds from hypothermia. But on his face was a big grin that said: I made it—and I can't wait to tell you about it.

For years, Pete had tried to persuade me to go with him to Alaska. I was tempted. It certainly looked stunning in his pictures. But his stories—about glaciers calving, water so cold it could kill you, being chased in his kayak by a sea lion, hikers falling into deep crevasses—also scared the hell out of me.

Pete was a risk taker. In the 1980s, he had founded an advertising agency in Cincinnati, our hometown. Early on, he nearly lost everything. Once he had to mortgage his house to pay his employees. He always put others first. I admired that.

But Pete stuck with it—and it worked. He built his company into Cincinnati's largest ad agency. It became *the* place to work, especially if you were young in the business. It wasn't just successful. It was hip. Employees brainstormed while shooting pool in a conference room, Pete right along with them. He might have been old enough to be their father. But the other dads didn't sport a goatee, dress in black, tweet and bring home from Cannes a Gold Lion, one of the advertising industry's most prestigious awards.

And Pete's years of hard work paid off. In 2005, he sold his company to the biggest ad agency in the world for a small fortune. Pete's risk was also his reward.

I, on the other hand, was not a risk taker. I worked in public relations for one of the most conservative companies in the world. In 2007, I had been there for 27 years.

And while Pete was diving into ice water and being chased by sea lions, I was busy defending the safety of the latest controversial ingredient in shampoo.

But as different as our lives were, as different as we were, Pete and I became the best of friends. Part of it, I think, is that we balanced each other out.

But there was something more. I think Pete and I also became good friends because we could just be ourselves with each other.

At work, and even at home, we had roles to play, important roles, roles we loved. But the more we got into these roles, the harder it was to get out of them, to find an escape hatch, a way to step out and let down, to talk freely, to share problems without feeling obliged to also propose solutions.

This was the safe haven that Pete and I found, a place where we could be unguarded and unvarnished, a place void of pretense, a place of vulnerability, a place of pure acceptance.

We met through our wives, who met through our children. But I don't remember ever meeting Pete. Suddenly, he was just there, and we were hanging out, running together, drinking wine and telling jokes. We went to movies, dinner and baseball and football games together. We played golf, badly, together. We argued a lot, especially over politics and religion. We talked or texted nearly every day. And at some point, without ever saying so, we became best friends.

Pete kept asking me to go to Alaska, and I kept saying no. We would have to go in July, he said, the only time it was warm enough. And every July, I'd have a good excuse.

But the truth is: I was wary. For starters, I'm a poor swimmer, and I'm uncomfortable in the water. I wasn't sure I could handle being on a little boat and paddling around in a sea kayak in ice water for a week.

But Pete never gave up. And finally, in 2007, I said yes. Even now, I'm not really sure why I gave in. Maybe Pete just wore me down. Or maybe, after decades of trying to control things, I decided it was time to let go.

Pete was thrilled and went into fast motion. Within 24 hours, he had booked everything—the boat, flights, ground transportation and a place where we'd spend our first night in a tiny town called Gustavus, about 40 miles from Juneau, on the Gulf of Alaska.

★

We met in the Seattle airport on a Saturday afternoon. Pete had flown in from Cincinnati. I had flown in from Myrtle Beach, where I had just spent a week on a family vacation. When I got there, I saw that Pete had sent a text message to tell me he was in the Seattle Tap Room in Concourse B.

Pete was a man of extremes. At times, he could drink a lot and drink fast. All told, we had a brief, seven-beer layover.

From Seattle, we flew to Juneau, another two and half hours north. The airport there is the size of a convenience store. We boarded an eight-passenger Cessna for the 20-minute flight to Gustavus.

We flew low the whole time. Just below, I saw rivers, lakes, lagoons, mountains and glaciers.

As we were about to land, I could finally see the bay. It was dark blue and narrower than I had expected. I'd seen rivers as wide. But it seemed to extend forever, separating and branching out through the snow-capped mountains, more like a web of rivers than a bay.

But what really grabbed my attention were the glaciers. For some reason, I had always had trouble wrapping my mind around the idea of glaciers. As a city boy, I used to confuse them with icebergs.

Pete set me straight. He explained that icebergs are chunks of ice that break off from glaciers. Many are big—like the one the Titanic hit. Some are tiny, the size of ice cubes. All glaciers, though, are huge. Some stretch for hundreds of miles. They move slowly through the mountains and valleys, scouring the earth, always advancing and retreating.

Still, I had a hard time envisioning them. But then, from the plane, I saw them. They looked nothing like icebergs. They were a confluence of white, blue and grey. They looked like great tentacles, snaking through the mountain ranges like giant, frozen rivers. Some of them stretched beyond my field of vision, even at 5,000 feet.

"There it is!" Pete exclaimed from his seat in front of me, pointing down at the bay. "Isn't it incredible?"

Good Lord, it was breathtaking—the most majestic landscape I'd ever seen. But it looked wild and daunting too, and I wondered what I had gotten myself into.

★

We landed on a runway that seemed far too short, descended the shaky aluminum stairs to the tarmac and grabbed our duffel bags from the belly of the plane. We slung them over our shoulders and lugged them through the tiny airport to the parking lot.

From there, a van took us to the inn, 10 minutes away. As soon as we left, I knew I was in a very special place.

The land was flat and rolled out in grassy prairies in every direction, surrounded by tall, dark evergreens rimmed by low, blue-green, snow-capped mountains in the distance. We passed a dozen houses, a few lodges, a school, a small general store, a library, two restaurants and a gas station with old-time, red pumps. The whole scene reminded me of one of those 1930s westerns that's been colorized.

Then suddenly we pulled into the long driveway of an inn.

It was large and white, two-storied, with a reddish-brown roof. I could tell from all the angles and windows that there were many rooms inside. The front lawn was 50 yards wide, and the grass smelled freshly cut. On one side stood a wall of towering, dark green fir trees. On the other, a rolling meadow of tall grasses and wildflowers.

Just beyond the meadow, extending behind the building, was a sprawling garden, with alternating rows of vegetables and flowers—pansies, fuchsia, petunias, carnations, marigolds, snapdragons, sweet-peas, poppies, lupines and geraniums—in waves of red, white, pink, lavender, blue, orange and yellow. I was surprised to see such a vibrant display of flowers in a climate so harsh.

A split-rail fence framed the back and one side of the garden, some of it covered by blackberry, raspberry and red currant bushes. The air smelled earthy and sweet, a blend of rhubarb, flowers and pines. Beyond the garden stood an orchard, whose trees marched single file into the woods at the base of a broad, low mountain, the backdrop to everything. It was a scene that was at once wild and tamed, natural and crafted.

The owners of the inn were gracious hosts. We ate very well that evening. After dinner, we sampled the local craft beers at a small bar next to the kitchen.

Even though it wasn't dark yet—in July, the sun doesn't set in Alaska until about 10 o'clock—we were exhausted. So we headed to our rooms. I closed the curtains to block the early sunrise, then slipped into bed.

★

My alarm went off at seven, but the hearty scents of bacon, eggs and coffee had already roused me.

I had slept like a man who had traveled 3,000 miles on a beer-of-the-month-club trip the day before. Still, I was tempted to snooze a little longer. But then, someone started banging on my door.

"Time for breakfast!" Pete shouted. I just knew his goofy face was scrunched up against my door.

"Get up, Don! We've got to be at the dock in an hour."

I was just stirring some blueberries into my oatmeal when folks began to get up, go to their rooms and check out. Soon, I was the only one left at the table—which was fine by me, since I was packed and ready to go.

I savored my oatmeal, buttered some toast, sipped my coffee and sat alone, facing two large windows along the back wall of the inn. The glass was thick—to withstand the harsh winters, I guessed. The garden flowers were brilliant in the morning sun, and they swayed in the breeze. And through the glass, awash with light, all the colors of the garden danced and blended together, like a kaleidoscope.

And I remembered it was Sunday. It felt like a Sunday morning in church. I knew it was cool outside. But with the sunlight streaming in, the air in the dining room was warm, and I felt radiant and so grateful for everything, including for Pete, for his persistence, for being there and for the courage to have finally said yes.

★

We boarded our small ship at a place called Bartlett Cove and set out for six days and six nights on Glacier Bay. There were nine passengers and five crew members. Our boat would cruise the bay by day and anchor in quiet coves at night. Most days, we went sea kayaking. Some days, we went hiking.

Now, on the first day, it was time to kayak. There were six kayaks in all: five two-man kayaks and a single for John, our guide.

"Let's go together, Don," Pete said. "You take the front, and I'll take the back."

I knew what that meant: Pete wanted to be in charge. I knew Pete was an experienced kayaker. He owned a kayak and took it out on a small lake near his house.

I didn't have nearly as much experience kayaking. But I had done a lot of canoeing as a kid. And I had done a couple of triathlons with Pete which included canoeing on the Little Miami River. I remembered he insisted on being in the back then too. We flipped our canoe about every mile.

"Are you sure?" I asked Pete.

"You worry too much," he replied. "Besides, we're wearing wetsuits."

Pete could be so confidence-inspiring.

"Hey, guys!" John yelled. "Don't go very far."

I'm glad he did because Pete had already started paddling away.

"Pete," I said. "John said to stay close."

"Don't worry," he replied. "I'm just getting us into position."

Pete liked to say that kind of crap, knowing it made absolutely no sense. I knew him, though. He just wanted to see how far he could go before John called us back.

"Hey, guys!" John yelled, as if on cue.

Pete stopped paddling. We glided to a stop.

I looked around. What had seemed big from the air, as we flew in yesterday, was now nearly too massive to comprehend.

Our boat had anchored in the middle of a narrow stretch of the bay. In front of me rose a glacier, stormy blue and powder white. It must have been 150 feet tall.

On the other side of the bay, behind us, stood a temperate rain forest. The tall evergreens were covered with mosses and lichens. I could see wildflowers and the trunks of downed trees along the forest floor. Streams flowed like fingers out of the woods, trickling down the rocky shore through brown moss-covered boulders and into the bay.

And surrounding everything were mountains that rose thousands of feet and stretched farther than I could see. The bay itself seemed endless too, like the ocean.

And there we were, Pete and I, in the center of all this, sitting in a 16-foot plastic kayak, floating, like a leaf on a pond, best friends, saying nothing, directing nothing, wanting nothing, just floating, immersed in a new world, a larger world, for a moment, this moment, together.

★

All six kayaks were now in the water. John reminded us to stick together. Then he pulled a large, expensive-looking Nikon camera from his kayak. He told us that in addition to being a tour guide, he was a professional photographer. He said he would be taking our pictures all week.

And with that, as a group, we headed toward an enormous glacier. The closer we got, the more ice I saw in the water. At first, it was in the form of tiny icebergs, no bigger than ice cubes.

"Grab one, Don," Pete said, leaning over and scooping one up in his hand. "Taste it," he said, popping it in his mouth and chomping on it like candy. "This is the oldest ice cube you'll ever have."

I reached out and snagged one. The water was freezing. The ice cube was clear and slick, and I could see small stone particles and air bubbles inside. I licked it and put it in my mouth. But with all that debris inside, I decided against biting it. It tasted clean. I guess I was expecting it to taste like salt—or dirt. I sucked on it for a minute, numbing my tongue. Then I spit it back into the sea.

We kept paddling toward the glacier. The icebergs were getting larger, some now the size of basketballs, others as big as cars. Some were square, some flat, some domed. Pete maneuvered us through them, the smallest ones bouncing off the sides of our kayak. Then, a few hundred yards from the glacier, John yelled: "Stop everybody!"

We all stopped paddling.

"Quiet," he said. "Listen. Just listen."

At first, I wasn't sure what he meant. Then I heard something popping, crackling, the sound echoing off the glacier.

"This glacier is melting," John told us. "Every glacier melts. But now they're melting faster than ever. That popping is the sound of air bubbles escaping from the ice. The ice is constantly melting, so that popping sound never stops."

Suddenly, we heard a much louder noise—like a clap of thunder. A huge chunk of ice had broken off the middle of the glacier in front of us. It slid down the face, leaving a cascade of snow and ice in its trail. The ice exploded into the water, creating a broad wave, which rolled toward us, slowly.

I looked around for John. He shouted not to worry, it wasn't a "big one." He said to just point our kayaks toward the wave and ride it. Pete re-oriented us, and I had to back paddle hard to give us enough time to square up. The first wave was now just seconds away.

"Hold on, Don," Pete said. "Here it comes!"

I watched as the wave hit us straight on, then felt it go under our boat, rocking us, front to back. It was like riding a kids' rollercoaster—except surrounded by about a million gallons of ice water. I pushed my paddle down hard against the top of our kayak to steady myself.

"Holy shit!" Pete shouted. "What a rush!"

"Thank God," I sighed, relieved we were still upright.

"I can't believe we saw calving on the first day," Pete said. "This is going to be a great trip!"

Everyone was hooting and hollering—and Pete and I hadn't flipped our boat. Maybe he knew what he was doing after all.

After checking out the glacier a bit more, but still at a safe distance, we all turned around and headed for the other shore. It was as lush as the other was frozen. On this side was an old-growth forest of massive hemlock and spruce trees. They stretched up and down the shore line as far as I could see-a rocky, jagged shore line, etched with inlets and coves.

For the next hour or so, we would explore several of those coves. Along the way, we began to see an astonishing array of wildlife. We saw sea otters with brown fur, the size of puppies, floating on their backs, looking surprisingly carefree. We saw several bald eagles. Until then, I'd never seen even one. We saw dozens of puffins, which John described perfectly as "flying potatoes." And near the shore, we looked down into the clear water and saw large red, blue, green, yellow, even purple, star-fish.

Pete and I began to drift away from the others, toward the center of the bay. We hadn't strayed far, but far enough to make me a little uneasy.

"Pete, let's stay with the group," I said.

"I'm keeping them in sight," Pete said. "We're fine. You worry too much."

Maybe he was right. Maybe I was worrying too much. Pete had been here twice before. He did seem to know what he was doing, and he hadn't steered me wrong so far. I guess I just needed to learn to relax.

Then suddenly, Pete cried: "Look! I think it's a sea lion!"

Oh God, I thought. I turned around to see Pete. He was pointing ahead to our left. I pivoted back around and looked out—and saw something big thrashing near the middle of the bay. It was less than 100 feet away.

"Let's go take a look," Pete said. I felt our kayak surge forward.

"Come on, Pete," I said. "Those things are dangerous."

"It's not going to bother us," he replied. "It's busy. It's eating lunch."

As we got closer, I realized it was indeed a sea lion. It was huge—I guessed maybe 10 feet long and 1,000 pounds. It was dark brown, with black fins, a small head, thick neck, flat nose, long whiskers and bulging black eyes.

I stopped paddling, but Pete didn't, and so we inched closer to the beast. I could see its mouth now—and its teeth: four long, curved canines in the front with rows of cone-shaped incisors behind. When I saw those teeth, "sea lion" suddenly made sense.

And it was indeed eating lunch. It had caught a king salmon. It probably weighed 30 pounds, but the sea lion tossed it high in the air, like a rag doll, tearing it apart. Blood and pieces of flesh and bone flew everywhere. And with each toss, the sea lion would take another bite of the fish, its head snapping back, like a ravenous dog chomping on a piece of raw meat.

"Pete, stop," I said in a loud whisper.

Now we were only about 20 feet away—close enough, apparently, even for Pete because he finally stopped paddling. We glided to a stop and just sat there, transfixed as the predator violently, powerfully devoured the last of its poor prey.

Then the beast looked at us, opened its mouth wide, made a deep, growling, menacing sound and slipped under the surface of the water.

"Hey, guys!" John yelled, breaking our trance. "Get back here!"

I turned around to see him. He and the other kayakers were 100 yards behind us.

Then I caught a glimpse of Pete. He was just sitting there, his paddle resting in front of him, with a big smile on his face.

He was quiet. Pete was seldom quiet. I think he was happy. I think he was happy that we had just witnessed something so wild and intense and that we hadn't kept our distance. I think he was happy that we had seen that glacier calve and ridden the wave. I think he was happy to have steered us through those icebergs. I think he was happy to be back in Alaska and showing me the ropes. And although he never said so, in that moment, I think Pete was very happy to be alive.

And I was happy too. I was happy to be guided for a change, to let go, to give up control. I was happy to leave my familiar world behind and enter this mysterious new one. I was happy to unplug. I was happy that this adventure was just beginning. I was happy at the prospect of not shaving for a week. And, of course, I was happy that I hadn't just been eaten by a sea lion.

★

The next morning, we all shuffled into the galley for breakfast. John was sitting at the end of the table, drinking coffee and bidding us good morning.

As we munched on bagels, he told us that this morning we would kayak to Margerie Glacier. There, we would paddle to shore near the edge of the glacier and eat lunch. Then we would hike up the side of a mountain which borders the glacier.

"If everybody's up for it, we should be able to climb up about 2000 feet and see about 10 miles of the bay," Dave said. "The view is spectacular!"

Two hours later, we were climbing that mountain. The trail was steep, narrow and very rocky. The brush—tall grasses and bushes—was coarse and thick. The climb was a struggle, and we had to stop several times to rest. But at about 2,000 feet, we reached a plateau. There, we all stopped and looked out over the bay.

John was right: we could see for miles. In the bright sun, the bay looked like a giant mirror. Everything was reflected in it—mountains, forests, glaciers, even the sky. Everything was revealed in the water.

The air was cool, and the wind bore the scent of everything below us: the trees, the rocks, the moss, the salt water, the ice. The fragrance of all these things rose up to meet us on the wind, and I closed my eyes and breathed it in.

And for a moment, I did not feel separate from these things. I felt one with them and everything. And I felt I had known this once, long ago—and that if I could be still and open, as I was at that moment, I could know it again.

★

That night, Pete and I lay awake for a while in our bunks. I told him about my experience on the mountain that day, about my feeling of communion with everything.

I thought he might laugh or start snoring. But he listened and said he had had a similar feeling himself—the last time he was in Alaska.

"I've never put it into words," he said. "But that's how I felt. I brought that feeling home with me, and I thought I'd never lose it. But I did. Now, though, I'm feeling it again. You're right. When you really think about it, it all begins to blend together."

Pete stopped talking, and I just listened. I thought maybe he had fallen asleep.

"Pete?"

"Yeah."

"Thanks."

"For what?"

"For bringing me here, for not giving up on me. For this whole thing."

"Sure," he said. "Good night, Don."

"Good night, Pete."

★

The next day, we "shot the arch," a massive arched iceberg carved by water, wind and time in a cove of the bay. The parabola-shaped opening was probably 50 feet tall but only about 20 feet wide. The water pulsed through it, tons of water, suddenly constrained and channeled, crashing violently against the walls of the arch in 10-foot surges. And when the water hit those walls, it sounded like thunder.

I could hardly imagine going through there in a kayak. But we all huddled around John in our kayaks near the entrance, and he told us how to do it. The trick, he said, is to stay in the middle, point your kayak toward the other end and just ride it.

"Don't try to steer or even paddle," he told us. "Just get out of the way and let it take you. Watch me."

Then, without hesitating, he showed us how by going first. Once we saw him ride the crest of those waves straight through, and come out alive, our spines stiffened—and everyone began lining up to go next.

Still, I knew this was not like any kayaking I had done in the past. And I now understood why John had made each of us bring a helmet that day. I fastened mine tight.

All week, Pete and I had kayaked together. Today, though, one of the crew members was my partner and another passenger was his. On one hand, I was sorry not to be doing this with Pete. But on the other, I got to watch him shoot the arch.

Pete and his new bowman were both big men. But going through the arch, with their helmets on, bobbing wildly, at the mercy of the waves, they looked like a couple of Fisher-Price little people in a toy boat.

Over the roar, I could hear their screams, echoing off the walls, screams of ecstasy, of pure joy, like children opening gifts on Christmas morning. Hearing that was as thrilling to me as my own turn through the arch.

And as I shot through, there was Pete waiting, cheering me on, looking as happy as I had ever seen him.

★

Friday would be our last day of sea kayaking.

We dropped anchor at a place in the bay called Adolphus Point. John told us it was a popular feeding spot for humpback whales. They spent their summers there, "rebuilding their blubber supply," he said, after migrating 3,000 miles every year from Hawaii, where they mate and have babies.

We had hoped to see one, but at a distance—and from the ship! And yet here we were, Pete and I, watching breathlessly from our kayak as three humpbacks headed straight toward us.

Side by side, one by one, they dove under the surface of the water, then emerged, like giant pistons. As they did, they blew great puffs of misty spray into the air. Their exhaling made a gushing sound, like steam blasting from a locomotive. Their backs were mottled black. They were now less than 100 yards away.

John yelled to us to tap our paddles on our kayak. Of course! During our orientation the first day, he had told us to do this if we ever saw a whale, no matter how far away, so it would know where we were and not accidentally upend us.

I felt so small and vulnerable. My heart raced. I had no options. All I could do was wait, tap my paddle and hope the whales would hear us.

Then, suddenly, they were gone. Fifty feet away, the whales disappeared.

"Where did they go?" I asked.

"Oh, shit!" Pete said. "I think they're under the boat!"

"Keep tapping!" John shouted. Pete and I tapped our paddles furiously.

Then suddenly, a whale burst through the surface of the water ten feet in front of me. Boom! It must have been 50 feet long. I could have reached out and touched it with my paddle. Its skin was bumpy, like a cucumber. It had a small fin on its back. Barnacles encrusted the underside of its mouth. Its eye was the size of a baseball. It looked like a gigantic human eye—and it was staring right at me.

Whoosh! The whale blew its spray hard and high into the air. The sound was so deep I could feel the vibration. Spray rained down on us. It tasted salty and fishy, like sardines.

Then a second whale burst through the surface, just to our left. Boom! Then a third, just to our right. Boom! They formed a crescent around us. And they were all blowing their spray into the air. We were soaked with it.

By now, it was clear the whales knew where we were, so Pete and I stopped tapping and just sat there and stared at them as they stared at us. They seemed content just to watch us and didn't come any closer. They hovered gracefully. I started breathing again.

And so there we were, the five of us, together, in a big ring in the sea. The whales began moaning, groaning, almost singing. It occurred to me that maybe they were communicating with each other. Or maybe with us.

A few moments ago, these enormous creatures had terrified me. But then, maybe out of desperation, I let go. And now, as I looked into their eyes, I was no longer afraid.

As Pete and I sat there, we did not speak. We had entered a wordless place, a place of stillness, a sacred place.

At some point, we realized that our friends were cheering. They had seen it all. And what Pete and I didn't know is that John had been taking pictures of us the whole time.

★

The next morning, after a late breakfast, our boat cruised into Bartlett Cove, where most of us had met just six days earlier. We were certainly not strangers now, though, and we didn't want to say goodbye.

A van was waiting at the dock to take us to the airport. But for a few minutes, we all lingered, hugging each other.

We promised to stay in touch. We said we'd see each other again. But we knew that wouldn't happen.

And it never did. Five years later, suddenly and unexpectedly, Pete died of a massive heart attack.

★

I've given up trying to make sense of Pete's death. But the more that time passes, and the more my specific memories of him fade and blur, the clearer I am on how our friendship changed me, how it opened and expanded me.

For me, our Alaska trip was the flashpoint.

There, I learned to let go, to let someone else steer. There, I remembered we are all connected and that I am not really separate from anything, not even the whales. There, I came to understand that that which had once seemed so foreign and even frightening to me had now become a part of me, just as it always had been.

I discovered these things in 2007 in Alaska with my friend Pete. He had waited for me a long time. He is waiting for me still.

But separation, I now know, is an illusion.

And so I close my eyes and see Pete, smiling in our kayak, chomping on a tiny iceberg, shooting the arch. I see him sitting in front of me on the plane, pointing down at Glacier Bay and saying: "Isn't it incredible?"

Photo by John Schnell

About the Author

After a long career in the corporate world, Don Tassone has returned to his creative writing roots, living his passion for the written word which first led him to earn a degree in English. *Sampler* is his fourth book. The others are Drive, a novel, and two other short story collections, *Get Back* and *Small Bites.* Don also teaches at Xavier University in Cincinnati. He and his wife Liz live in Loveland, Ohio. They have four children.

Made in the USA
Lexington, KY
06 November 2019

56499672R00083